DOVER·THRIFT·EDITIONS

Cyrano de Bergerac

EDMOND ROSTAND

Translated by
LOUIS UNTERMEYER

DOVER PUBLICATIONS, INC.
Mineola, New York

DOVER THRIFT EDITIONS

GENERAL EDITOR: PAUL NEGRI
EDITOR OF THIS VOLUME: JOSLYN T. PINE

Bibliographical Note

This Dover edition of *Cyrano de Bergerac*, first published in 2000, is an unabridged, slightly corrected republication of the text of the Louis Untermeyer blank verse translation, originally published by The Heritage Press, New York in 1954.

Library of Congress Cataloging-in-Publication Data

Rostand, Edmond, 1868–1918.
   [Cyrano de Bergerac. English]
   Cyrano de Bergerac / Edmond Rostand ; translated by Louis Untermeyer.
      p. cm.
   Unabridged republication of the text of the Louis Untermeyer blank verse translation, originally published by the Heritage Press in 1954.
   ISBN 0-486-41119-2 (pbk.)
      1. Cyrano de Bergerac, 1619–1655—Drama. I. Untermeyer, Louis, 1885–1977.
II. Title.

PQ2635.O72 C92 2000
842'.8—dc21

99-087751

Manufactured in the United States of America
Dover Publications, Inc., 31 East 2nd Street, Mineola, N.Y. 11501

Note

EDMOND ROSTAND (1868–1918) was a French dramatist born in Marseilles to a wealthy and cultured family. His father was an accomplished journalist and translator of Catullus who encouraged his son's natural inclination toward literature. Rostand excelled at his studies, and was thoroughly schooled in the Greek and Latin classics, as well as in the history, language and literature of France. It has been said by some scholars that, among foreign authors, only Shakespeare and Goethe received his careful attention. Young Edmond wrote poetry and plays at an early age as if a romantic career was his birthright. At the age of twenty-two, he married the poetess Rosemonde Gérard and presented her with his first published book, *Les Musardises*, a volume of verse. Although largely derivative, it nonetheless exhibited sparks of the genius that would later ignite in the creation of his greatest work, *Cyrano de Bergerac*. After his marriage in 1890, the couple settled in Paris where Rostand frequented theatrical circles, eventually winning the friendship of the distinguished romantic actor, Constant Coquelin, for whom he would later write the role of Cyrano.

In 1892, *The Two Pierrots*—Rostand's farce in one act—was presented at the Comédie Française. It was well-reviewed and received as a delightful little comedy which was to remain in the French repertoire as a curtain-raiser. Two years later he would have his first real artistic and financial success with *The Romancers*, a satirical fantasy. At the age of twenty-seven, he wrote *The Faraway Princess* for the fabled actress Sarah Bernhardt, who produced and acted the title role in her own theatre. When the Dreyfus affair inspired a political controversy that inflamed France, Rostand sided with his compatriots Zola, Proust, and Anatole France in favor of the Jewish army captain accused of proffering French secrets to the Germans. Despite the furor, and within the same time frame, he also managed to complete two plays: *The Woman of Samaria* and *Cyrano de Bergerac*, which was the pinnacle of his career. Three more plays followed, none of which would replay the glory of the latter.

The character of Cyrano was real: the original was a 17th-century poet and soldier who was a contemporary of Molière. Savinien Cyrano de Bergerac (1619–1655) was born in Paris. Possessed of a critical and creative spirit, he rebelled against the routine education of his youth. On the loose in Paris, he lived a rather wild life and—as legend has it—delighted in his enormous nose and fought more than a thousand duels in defense of it. He eventually enlisted in the noble guards about 1638, where he exhibited a reckless bravery, the war in Flanders giving him the opportunity to show his courage in service for his king. He gave up his military career when he failed to receive a promotion, and henceforth devoted himself to study and writing. De Bergerac wrote plays, succeeding in drama as well as farce; the highly praised *Death of Agrippina* was said to be his favorite. Other writings included novels about imaginary trips to the moon and the sun, and about the nature of the inhabitants. Considered the forerunners of books such as Swift's *Gulliver's Travels* and Voltaire's *Micromégas*, these works are a curious mixture of philosophy, imaginative science and satire. Sadly, his life had a tragic end, not retold in the Rostand play: whether by accident or an act of malicious intent, a large piece of timber fell on him; the episode seriously impaired his health, and he suffered terribly for a year before he died at the age of thirty-six. According to his lifelong friend, mentor and biographer Henri Le Bret, what was notable about de Bergerac (besides his big nose) was his wit, his learning, his respect for women, his fearless deeds and his integrity. Edmond Rostand selected out the details from his hero's life that best served his own dramatic conception.

Rostand's play, *Cyrano de Bergerac*, opened to wide acclaim on December 28, 1897, when the playwright was only twenty-nine years old. As its star Constant Coquelin tells it:

> The first night was eagerly awaited by the critics, the literary, and the artistic worlds. The audience that night was undoubtedly the cream of our Parisian public. When the curtain rose on the first act there was not a seat vacant in the theatre. The emotion of a great event was floating in the air. Never, never have I lived through such a night. . . . There is but one phrase to express the enthusiasm of our first performance—'a house in delirium' alone gives any idea of what took place. As the curtains fell on each succeeding act the entire audience would rise to its feet, shouting and cheering for ten minutes at a time. . . . I was trembling so that I could hardly get from one costume into another, and had to refuse my door to every one. Amid all this confusion Rostand alone seemed unconscious of his victory.

Thereafter, *Cyrano de Bergerac* became an integral piece of theatre history, translated into every European language as well as several Oriental tongues. There have been numerous English versions, including Howard Thayer Kingsbury's version that was presented to New York audiences in 1898—less than a year after its Paris debut. There was a comic opera made from the play in 1899, also performed in New York, with music by Victor Herbert. And much later, in the 1940s, a revival was staged by José Ferrer who would also star in the 1950 film adaptation. In 1987 the movie *Roxanne*, a Steve Martin vehicle, presented a modernized rendition of the story. And in 1990, there was yet another more traditional French screen version of *Cyrano de Bergerac* starring Gérard Depardieu.

Characters in the Play

THE MEN:

CYRANO DE BERGERAC
CHRISTIAN DE NEUVILLETTE
THE COUNT DE GUICHE
RAGUENEAU
LE BRET
CAPTAIN CARBON DE CASTEL-JALOUX
THE CADETS
LIGNIERE
VISCOUNT DE VALVERT
A MARQUIS
SECOND MARQUIS
THIRD MARQUIS
MONTFLEURY, THE ACTOR
BELLEROSE
JODELET
CUIGY
BRISSAILLE

A BUSYBODY
A MUSKETEER
ANOTHER MUSKETEER
A SPANISH OFFICER
A LIGHT GUARDSMAN
THE DOORKEEPER
A TRADESMAN
HIS SON
A PICKPOCKET
A SPECTATOR
A GUARD
BERTRANDOU, THE FIFER
A CAPUCHIN MONK
TWO MUSICIANS
THE POETS
THE PASTRY-COOKS

THE WOMEN:

ROXANE
HER DUENNA
LISE
THE ORANGE GIRL
MOTHER MARGARET DE JESUS
SISTER MARTHA

SISTER CLAIRE
AN ACTRESS
A SOUBRETTE
THE PAGES
THE FLOWER GIRL

THE CROWD, *Tradesmen, Marquises, Musketeers, Pickpockets, Pastry-Cooks, Poets, Gascon Cadets, Actors, Violinists, Pages, Children, Spanish Soldiers, Spectators, Bluestockings, Actresses, Nuns, etc.*

THE FIRST FOUR ACTS TAKE PLACE IN 1640; THE FIFTH IN 1655

Act I

A Performance at the Hotel Burgundy

THE HALL *of the Hotel Burgundy in 1640. It is built in the shape of a tennis court, but is arranged and decorated for a theatrical performance.*

The hall is oblong. It is seen diagonally, so that one of its sides forms part of the background and makes an angle to the entrance on the left. There it meets the stage itself—a small stage within a stage—which is seen obliquely. There are benches on both sides of this stage. There is a curtain, made of two tapestries which can be drawn aside. There is a small proscenium, above which the royal arms are displayed. Broad steps lead from the stage to the floor; on either side of these steps are places for the musicians. The footlights are candles.

There are two rows of side galleries; the upper one is divided into boxes. There are no seats on the floor of the hall (the pit) which is the real stage of the theatre. At the back of the pit—that is, in the right foreground—there is a staircase which leads to the gallery, and there is a buffet-sideboard with two small candelabras, a vase of flowers, fruit, cakes, bottles, etc.

The entrance to the hall is in the middle background, to the right of the spectators. The large door, which opens to admit the stage audience, is under the gallery. On the panels of the door, and over the buffet, there are red placards on which are printed the name of the play to be given this evening: "La Clorise."

At the rise of the curtain—the large curtain of the theatre itself—the hall is empty. The chandeliers, not yet lighted, are lowered in the middle of the pit.

The stage audience, the general public, begins to arrive. Little by little they assemble: Soldiers, Gentlemen, Tradesmen, Lackeys, Pages, Pickpockets, the Doorkeeper. These are followed by the Marquises, the Orange Girl who serves at the buffet, the Musicians, Cuigy, Brissaille.

Loud voices are heard outside the door. A Musketeer enters hurriedly.

THE DOORKEEPER.   Hi there! Your fifteen sous!

THE MUSKETEER.   I get in free.

THE DOORKEEPER.   How so?

THE MUSKETEER.   I'm in the Royal Cavalry.

THE DOORKEEPER [*to another who has entered*].   And you?

SECOND MUSKETEER.   No payment. I'm a musketeer.

FIRST MUSKETEER [*to the second*].
> Look here, the play does not begin till two.
> The pit is empty. Let us try our foils. [*They fence.*]

A LACKEY [*entering*].   Pst—Flanquin!

ANOTHER LACKEY.   Champagne here?

FIRST LACKEY [*drawing cards and dice from his doublet*].
> Cards! Dice! Let's play.
> [*He sits down on the floor and is joined by the* SECOND LACKEY.]

SECOND LACKEY.   Right-o, you rogue.

FIRST LACKEY [*He takes a candle from his pocket, lights it, and sticks it on the wooden floor.*]   My master's candle-end;
> Just right for us—he won't make light of it.

A GUARDSMAN [*to a* FLOWER GIRL *coming in*].   Good girl, to come before the lights are lit. [*He puts his arm around her waist.*]

ONE OF THE MUSKETEERS [*fencing*].   Touché!

ONE OF THE LACKEYS.   Ha—clubs!

THE GUARDSMAN [*pursuing the girl*].   A kiss!

THE FLOWER GIRL.   Someone may see.

THE GUARDSMAN [*leading her to a dark corner*].   No danger here.

A MAN [*seating himself on the floor along with others who have brought a light lunch*].   Coming before the show,
> I always find time for a bite to eat.

A TRADESMAN [*enters with his young son*].   Let us sit here, my son.

ONE OF THE LACKEYS.   A pair of aces!

A MAN [*taking a bottle from under his cloak and sitting down with the others*].   A man who cares about his burgundy
> Should drink it at the Burgundy Hotel.

THE TRADESMAN [*to his son*].
> The theatre's fallen on evil days. You'd think
> We'd come to some disreputable place!
> [*He points to the drinker with the tip of his cane.*]
> Drunkards! [*He is jostled by one of the fencers.*]
> Fighters! [*He stumbles among the card-players.*]
> Gamblers!

THE GUARDSMAN [*behind him, in a teasing struggle with the girl*].
> One little kiss!

THE TRADESMAN [*pulling his son away*].

Good God! To think that in a hall like this
They used to play Rotrou!

THE YOUNG MAN.   And Corneille, too!

A GROUP OF PAGES [*entering, hand in hand, singing and dancing*].
Tra la la la la la la la la . . .

THE DOORKEEPER [*severely*].   No nonsense, boys!

FIRST PAGE [*with wounded dignity*].   Sir, what a thing to say! [*quickly, as soon as the doorkeeper turns away, to the* SECOND PAGE]
Did you bring string?

SECOND PAGE.   Yes, and a fish-hook, too.

FIRST PAGE.   Up in the gallery we can fish for wigs.

A PICKPOCKET [*drawing around him several hard-looking fellows*].
Now watch me closely, all you amateurs;
Here's the first course in How to Be a Thief . . .

SECOND PAGE [*calling to other* PAGES *who are already in the gallery*].
You there! Have you pea-shooters?

THIRD PAGE [*from above*].   Yes, and peas. [*He proves it by pelting the others.*]

THE YOUNG MAN [*to his father*].   What is the play?

THE TRADESMAN.   "Clorise."

THE YOUNG MAN.   Who wrote the work?

THE TRADESMAN.   Balthasar Baro. It's his masterpiece.
[*Walks off, taking his son's arm*]

THE PICKPOCKET [*to his pupils*].
Breeches and sleeves are tricky. First of all
Look out for lace—be quick to cut it off.

A SPECTATOR [*pointing to the gallery*].
The first night of "The Cid" I was up there.

THE PICKPOCKET [*gesticulating*].   You lift the watches slowly . . .

THE TRADESMAN [*returning with his son*].   You will see
Some celebrated actors in the play . . .

THE PICKPOCKET [*with stealthy gestures*].   Handkerchiefs, thus . . .

THE TRADESMAN.   Montfleury . . .

A VOICE [*from the gallery*].   Light the lights!

THE TRADESMAN [continuing to list the actors].   Bellerose . . . l'Épy
. . . la Beaupré . . . Jodelet . . .

A PAGE.   Look, everyone! Here comes the Orange Girl.

THE ORANGE GIRL [*at her stand behind the buffet*].   Oranges! Milk!
Fruit syrup! Lemonade! [*A loud noise at the door*]

A FALSETTO VOICE.   Make room there, beasts!

A LACKEY [*in surprise*].   Marquises! In the pit?

ANOTHER LACKEY [*ironically*].   Just for an entrance.

[*Enter a group of overdressed* MARQUISES]

A MARQUIS [*observing the hall half-empty*].   What! Do we come in
　　Without disturbing anyone, like tradesmen,
　　Stepping on no one's toes! Fie! Fie for shame!
　　[*He recognizes other gentlefolk who have entered before.*]
　　Cuigy! Brissaille! [*General embracing*]
CUIGY.   The old guard's here once more;
　　Always before the hall is quite lit up.
THE MARQUIS.   Don't say lit up! I'm in a sickening mood—
ANOTHER MARQUIS.   Compose yourself, Marquis . . . Let there be
　　light!
THE AUDIENCE [*greeting the lamplighter*].   Ahhh! . . .

　　[*Groups gather around the chandelier while the candles are lit.
　　Some take seats in the galleries.* LIGNIÈRE *enters the pit, arm in arm
　　with* CHRISTIAN DE NEUVILLETTE. LIGNIÈRE *is somewhat di-
　　sheveled; he looks dissipated but, nevertheless, distinguished.*
　　CHRISTIAN, *on the other hand, is faultlessly dressed, if not quite in
　　the latest fashion. He seems preoccupied and keeps his eyes on the
　　boxes.*]

CUIGY.   Lignière!
BRISSAILLE [*laughing*].   Still sober, Lignière?
LIGNIERE [*sotto voce to* CHRISTIAN].   Shall I present you?
　　[CHRISTIAN *nods assent.*]
　　Baron de Neuvillette. [*He bows. The audience greets the rise of the
　　first illuminated chandelier with a long drawn-out "Ahhh!"*]
CUIGY [*to* BRISSAILLE, *indicating* CHRISTIAN].   A charming head.
FIRST MARQUIS [*who has overheard*].   Pooh!
LIGNIERE [*introducing* CHRISTIAN].   Messieurs de Cuigy,
　　De Brissaille. Friends . . .
CHRISTIAN [*bowing*].   Delighted.
FIRST MARQUIS [*murmuring to the* SECOND].   Passable.
　　Good-looking in a way—but out of style.
LIGNIERE [*to* CUIGY].   Christian has just come up from the Touraine.
CHRISTIAN.   Yes, I have been in Paris scarce three weeks;
　　Tonight's my last. Tomorrow I will join
　　The Guards, to serve with the Cadets.
FIRST MARQUIS [*watching the people entering the boxes*].   President
　　Aubry's wife!
THE ORANGE GIRL.   Oranges! Milk! [*The violins tune up.*]
CUIGY [*calling* CHRISTIAN'S *attention to the fact that the hall is filling
　　up*].   A huge crowd.

CHRISTIAN.   Yes.
FIRST MARQUIS.   The great world—and his wife.

[*They whisper the names of the women who, resplendently attired,
enter the boxes. Smiles and bows are exchanged.*]

SECOND MARQUIS.   Mesdames de Guéménée . . .
CUIGY.   De Bois-Dauphin . . .
FIRST MARQUIS.   With whom we're all in love . . .
BRISSAILLE.   De Chavigny . . .
SECOND MARQUIS.   Who toys with all our hearts . . .
LIGNIERE.   Ah, by the way, I see Corneille
    Is up from Rouen.
THE YOUNG MAN [*to his father*].   Has the Academy come?
THE TRADESMAN.   Certainly. There are many members here.
    There's Boudu, Boissat, and Cureau de Chambre,
    With Porchères, Colomby, Bourzeys, Bourdon,
    Arbaud . . . All names not one of which will die!
    How wonderful it is!
FIRST MARQUIS.   Attention! Now the *Précieuses* arrive;
    Those delicate, sophisticated ladies,
    Remote and magical: Barthénoïde,
    Urimédonte, Cassandace, Felixérie . . .
SECOND MARQUIS.   Their very names make music. Do you know
    Any of them?
FIRST MARQUIS.   Any? I know them all!
LIGNIERE [*taking* CHRISTIAN *aside*].
    Friend, I came here to do a favor. But
    The looked-for lady does not come. And so
    I go back to my vices, if you please.
CHRISTIAN [*pleading*].   No, no! You are the singer of the court
    As well as of the town—you are the one
    To tell me who she is, the fair unknown
    For whom I die each day. Stay, stay a while.
THE FIRST VIOLIN [*striking his bow on the stand*].   Now, gentlemen . . .
THE ORANGE GIRL.   Lemonade! Macaroons!

[*The violins begin playing.*]

CHRISTIAN.   I fear she is a wit or a coquette,
    And I am far from bright; I grope for words.
    The kind of language people use today
    Puzzles me. I'm a good soldier—but afraid . . .
    That's where she sits—the empty box up there—
    There on the right.

LIGNIERE.   D'Assoucy's waiting for me at the inn.
   I'd die of thirst here.
THE ORANGE GIRL [*passing with a tray*].   Fruit juice?
LIGNIERE.   Faugh!
THE ORANGE GIRL.   Milk?
LIGNIERE.   Pooh!
THE ORANGE GIRL.   Muscatel?
LIGNIERE.   Hm—I'll stay a little longer.
   Let's test this wine, my friend.
   [*He sits down by the buffet as the girl fills his glass.*]
THE AUDIENCE [*hailing a newcomer, a plump and jolly little fellow*].
   Ah! Ragueneau!
LIGNIERE.   That's the famed tavern-keeper, Ragueneau.
RAGUENEAU [*dressed in a pastry-cook's best Sunday clothes, walks quickly
   up to* LIGNIÈRE].   Sir, have you seen Monsieur de Bergerac?
LIGNIERE [*presenting* RAGUENEAU].
   The pastry-cook of actors—more than that,
   The patron saint of poets!
RAGUENEAU.   Monsieur, please!
   You do me too much honor.
LIGNIERE.   Oh, be still,
   Maecenas that you are!
RAGUENEAU.   Well, I'll admit
   That poets are my customers—
LIGNIERE.   On credit!
   And he himself writes gifted poetry.
RAGUENEAU.   A verse or two, perhaps.
LIGNIERE.   Mad about rhyme!
RAGUENEAU.   It's true that for a little ode—
LIGNIERE.   He'd give a pie!
RAGUENEAU.   Oh, just a little tart.
LIGNIERE.   Come, tell the truth!
   And for a triolet what would you give?
RAGUENEAU.   A finger roll.
LIGNIERE [*severely*].   A milk roll, nothing less!
   And you're attracted to the theatre?
RAGUENEAU.   I adore it!
LIGNIERE.   And the entrance price
   You pay with cakes! Your place tonight,
   Whisper it in my ear, cost you how much?
RAGUENEAU.   Four custards; fifteen cream-puffs . . . Cyrano
   Has not arrived?
LIGNIERE.   What then?

RAGUENEAU. Montfleury plays!

LIGNIERE. Why, to be sure, Montfleury plays tonight;
   The old wine-barrel acts the part of Phédon.
   But what has that to do with Cyrano?

RAGUENEAU. What! Don't you know? Cyrano hates the man
   And has forbidden him to speak a line
   On any stage, regardless, for a month.

LIGNIERE [*downing his fourth drink*]. So then?

RAGUENEAU. Montfleury plays tonight, unless . . .

CUIGY [*who has come up with his friends*]. Cyrano cannot stop him.

RAGUENEAU. That is what
   I've come to see.

FIRST MARQUIS. Who is this Cyrano?

CUIGY. A brilliant swordsman who knows every trick.

SECOND MARQUIS. Noble?

CUIGY. Noble enough. He's a Cadet,
   One of the Gascon Guards. But here's his friend
   Le Bret. He'll tell you everything. [CUIGY *calls to him.*] Le Bret!
   Looking for Cyrano?

LE BRET [*comes forward*]. Yes. I am worried.

CUIGY. Is the man really so extraordinary?

LE BRET [*with frank tenderness*].
   He is the rarest, choicest soul on earth.

RAGUENEAU. A poet!

CUIGY. Warrior!

BRISSAILLE. A philosopher!

LE BRET. Musician, too!

LIGNIERE. And what a sight he is!

RAGUENEAU. No painter could portray him. Jacques Callot
   Might have found place for him in some mad masque—
   An odd swashbuckler, fierce and fabulous,
   Bizarre, excessive and extravagant.
   He swaggers in a hat with three great plumes;
   His doublet is puffed out and sports six tails;
   His challenging sword-point lifts his cloak as high
   As though it were an insolent cock's tail,
   Pompous and impudent. He's prouder than
   The boldest rakehells of all Gascony . . .
   And, last but scarcely least, above his ruff
   He wears a nose, my lords. And what a nose!
   Seen for the first time, one cries out,
   "No, no! It is not true. The thing is false!
   Exaggerated! Unbelievable!"

And then one smiles and says, "It is a joke.
Soon he will take it off." But this, alas,
Is something Cyrano will never do.
LE BRET.   He keeps it on—it's death to mention it.
RAGUENEAU [*proudly*].   His sword is half of the dread shears of Fate.
FIRST MARQUIS [*shrugging*].   He will not come.
RAGUENEAU.   He'll come. I'll wager you
    A chicken à la Ragueneau.
FIRST MARQUIS [*smiling*].   Agreed.

[*Murmurs of admiration run through the hall.* ROXANE *appears,
seating herself in the front of her box; her duenna sits behind her.
Occupied in paying* THE ORANGE GIRL, CHRISTIAN *does not see
her.*]

SECOND MARQUIS [*with pretty little exclamations of joy*].
    Ah! Is she not too exquisite—too too
    Adorable!
FIRST MARQUIS.   She is a flawless peach
    With the faint perfume of a strawberry.
SECOND MARQUIS.   So fresh and cool that if you come too near
    You'll catch your death of cold.
CHRISTIAN [*raises his head, sees* ROXANE, *and suddenly seizes* LIGNIÈRE's
    arm].   Look! There she is!
LIGNIERE [*glancing up*].   Oh! Is it she?
CHRISTIAN.   Quickly—I am afraid.
LIGNIERE [*sipping his drink*].
    Madeleine Robin—called Roxane—well-born—
    A wit—
CHRISTIAN.   Alas!
LIGNIERE.   Unmarried—orphaned—and
    A cousin of the man of whom we spoke,
    Cyrano.

[*During this speech an elegantly dressed nobleman has entered. He
wears a blue ribbon, the Order of the Holy Ghost, on his breast, and
stands talking to* ROXANE.]

CHRISTIAN [*starting*].   Ah! And who is that—that man?
LIGNIERE [*winking tipsily*].
    Ha! That's the Count de Guiche. In love with her,
    But wedded to the niece of Richelieu.
    Wants her to marry Monsieur de Valvert,
    A viscount, old and dull—and *so* complaisant—
    Who'd look the other way. She won't agree.

But Count de Guiche is powerful. He knows
How to persuade an inexperienced girl.
I know his tricks. I have disclosed his plan;
Exposed it in a song which—when he hears—
Will make him flush with rage . . . Listen to this . . . [*He staggers
to his feet and clears his throat.*]

CHRISTIAN.   No thanks. Good night.

LIGNIERE.   What's wrong? Where would you go?

CHRISTIAN.   To meet Viscount de Valvert.

LIGNIERE.   Watch yourself!
The man will kill you! . . . Wait—*she's* watching you. [*He indicates*
ROXANE *with the flicker of an eye.*]

CHRISTIAN.   It's true—I'll stay. [CHRISTIAN *stands transfixed, looking
at her. The pickpockets notice his abstraction and draw close to
him.*]

LIGNIERE.   I am the one who goes.
I'm thirsty—and my friends are wondering
What has become of me . . . [*He reels out.*]

LE BRET [*who has been looking around the hall, breathes a sigh of relief
to* RAGUENEAU:].   No Cyrano.

RAGUENEAU [*incredulously*].   Nevertheless . . .

LE BRET.   Perhaps he has not seen
The playbill for tonight.

THE AUDIENCE.   Begin! Begin!

[DE GUICHE *comes down from* ROXANE's *box, crosses the pit, and is
immediately surrounded by a group of obsequious lordlings, including the* VISCOUNT DE VALVERT.]

FIRST MARQUIS.   This Count de Guiche has quite a following!

SECOND MARQUIS.   Another Gascon!

FIRST MARQUIS.   A Gascon, cold,
Subtle and keen . . . Let's pay him our respects.
[*They go towards* DE GUICHE.]

SECOND MARQUIS.   What lovely ribbons! What's the color called?
"Kiss-Me-My-Darling" or "Breast-of-a-Fawn?"

DE GUICHE.   The color's called "Sick Spaniard."

FIRST MARQUIS.   A good name.
The color tells the truth. For, thanks to you,
Things will go ill for Spain in Flanders fields.

DE GUICHE.   I'm going on the stage. Come on. [*As the* MARQUISES
and other lords follow him, he calls to the VISCOUNT:] Valvert.

CHRISTIAN [*hearing the name*].   Valvert! I'll throw right in his face

my— [*He reaches in his pocket and encounters the fingers of a thief.*] What!
THE PICKPOCKET.   Oh!
CHRISTIAN [*holding him*].   I was looking for a glove.
THE PICKPOCKET [*with a sickly smile*].   Instead,
    You find a hand. Pray, let it go. [*Changing his tone, he speaks softly but with great urgency.*] There is
    A secret I could tell you.
CHRISTIAN [*still holding him*].   Well?
THE PICKPOCKET.   Lignière—
    Your friend who has just left—
CHRISTIAN.   Go on.
THE PICKPOCKET.   —is near his end,
    A song of his has angered some great lord
    And now, tonight, a hundred men—I'm one—
    Will wait for him.
CHRISTIAN.   A hundred! Hired by whom?
THE PICKPOCKET.   Sorry. A secret.
CHRISTIAN [*with a shrug*].   Ha!
THE PICKPOCKET [*with great dignity*].   Professional!
CHRISTIAN.   Where do they wait?
THE PICKPOCKET.   Close to the Porte de Nesle.
    He'll have to go that way. He should be warned.
CHRISTIAN [*releasing him*].   Where is he now?
THE PICKPOCKET.   Try all the taverns. Try
    "The Golden Wine-Press," then "The Pine Cone," then
    "The Bursting Belt," "Two Torches," and "The Sign
    Of the Three Funnels." Leave a note
    In every one to warn him.
CHRISTIAN.   I must go!
    A hundred against one man! Cowards all! [*He looks lovingly at* ROXANE.] To leave her here! [*angrily in the direction of* VALVERT]
    And he—! But I must save
    Lignière. [*He rushes out.*]

[DE GUICHE, VALVERT, THE MARQUISES, *and the other lords have disappeared behind the curtain to seat themselves on the chairs at the sides of the little stage. The hall is full; the pit is crowded. There is not a vacant seat in the boxes and galleries.*]

THE AUDIENCE.   Begin! Begin!
THE TRADESMAN [*whose wig is suddenly drawn up, hooked by one of the* PAGES *in the upper gallery*].   My wig!
SHOUTS AND LAUGHTER.   He's bald!

One of the pages! Well done, boys! Bravo!

THE TRADESMAN [*shaking his fist*].   The little ruffians!

   SHOUTS AND LAUGHTER [*beginning very loud, then dying away*]
   Ha! Ha! Ha! Ha! Ha! Ha!

[*complete silence*]

LE BRET [*speaking to one of the spectators*].   What now? This sudden
   silence—[*The spectator whispers.*]
   Is it true?

THE SPECTATOR.   I have it on the best authority.

MURMURS IN THE AUDIENCE.   Hush! . . . Is it he? . . . No . . . Yes . . .
   The curtained box . . .
   He's there! . . . The Cardinal! . . .

A PAGE.   The devil! Now
   We'll have to be more careful. No more fun.

A MARQUIS [*unseen, behind the curtain*].   That candle should be
   snuffed.

ANOTHER MARQUIS [*also on stage, putting his head through an opening
   in the curtain*].   A chair!

[*A chair is passed up to him.* THE MARQUIS *takes it, kissing his
hand to the boxes.*]

A SPECTATOR.   Be still!

[*The traditional three knocks are heard on the stage. The curtains
part.* THE MARQUISES *are nonchalantly seated on the sides of the
stage. The painted backdrop depicts a quiet-colored pastoral land-
scape. Four small chandeliers cast their yellow light upon the stage.
The violins play softly.*]

LE BRET [*whispering to* RAGUENEAU].   Montfleury—will he dare?

RAGUENEAU [*also in a whisper*].   He's ready now;
   Clearing his throat.

LE BRET.   Cyrano is not here.

RAGUENEAU.   And I have lost my bet.

LE BRET.   So much the better.

[*An air is heard, played on a pastoral oboe, and* MONTFLEURY *appears upon the little stage. He is a huge man, and his bulk is ac-
centuated by the absurdity of his costume. He wears a shepherd's
smock; a hat, wreathed with roses, which droops over one ear; and
he is blowing on a drone-pipe tricked out with many ribbons.*]

THE AUDIENCE [*applauding*].   Bravo, Montfleury! Montfleury, bravo!

MONTFLEURY [*playing the part of* PHÉDON, *smirks, bows and begins*].

"Happy the man who dwells in solitude,
Far from the Court, in some sequestered mood;
Who, when sweet Zephyr whispers through the wood—"

A VOICE [*from the middle of the pit*].
Knave! Did I not forbid you to appear
For thirty days!

[*Everyone turns about. Murmurs run through the hall.*]

DIFFERENT VOICES.   Hey! . . . Really! . . . What is that?

[*People in the boxes stand up to get a better view.*]

CUIGY.   There—it is he!
LE BRET.   Cyrano!
THE VOICE.   King of clowns!
   Off stage at once!
THE ENTIRE AUDIENCE.   Oh!
MONTFLEURY.   But—
THE VOICE.   Are you still here!
DIFFERENT VOICES [*in the audience*].   Go on, Montfleury . . . Act . . .
   Don't be afraid . . .
MONTFLEURY [*ill at ease*].   "Happy the man who dwells in solitude—"
THE VOICE [*with menace*].   Monarch of misfits! Must I plant a wood,
   A forest on your back?

[*A heavy cane is flourished above the heads of the spectators.*]

MONTFLEURY [*his voice quavering*].   "Happy the man—"

[*The cane is shaken violently.*]

THE VOICE.   Get off!
THE AUDIENCE.   Oh! Oh!
MONTFLEURY [*gasping*].   "Happy the man who dwells—"
CYRANO [*Rising from the pit, he mounts a chair. His hat is cocked
   fiercely; his moustache bristles; his nose is frightening.*] Ah—I shall
   grow angry. [*Sensation*]
MONTFLEURY [*appealing to* THE MARQUISES].   Come to my aid.
A MARQUIS [*nonchalantly*].   Go on and act.
CYRANO.   Tub, if you do I'll break in all your staves!
THE MARQUIS.   Enough!
CYRANO.   Let the Marquis compose himself,
   Or my rough cane will spoil his dainty lace.
ALL THE MARQUISES [*rising indignantly*].   This is too much!
   Montfleury—
CYRANO.   Let him go!

I'll slit his ears and slice him if he stays!

A VOICE.   But—

CYRANO.   Go! I say!

ANOTHER VOICE.   But yet—

CYRANO.   Is he still here! [*He turns back his cuffs.*]
Good! I will make a sideboard of the stage
And carve this ripe, old sausage piece by piece!

MONTFLEURY [*as dignified as possible*].   When you insult me, you
insult The Muse!

CYRANO [*with extreme politeness*].
Sir, if the Muse, to whom you dare refer,
Who never heard your name, ever should meet
Such a great, greasy bowl of fat as you,
She'd greet you with her sandals—on your rear!

THE AUDIENCE.   Montfleury! Montfleury! Play Baro's play!

CYRANO   [*to those who are shouting*].
If you keep on, you'll rouse my sleeping sword
Out of its quiet scabbard. So—take care!

[*The crowd around him draws back.*]

THE CROWD.   Beware of him! Look out there!

CYRANO [*to* MONTFLEURY].   Leave the stage!

THE CROWD [*muttering*].   Oh! Oh!

CYRANO [*suddenly turning*].   Come on! Let's see just who objects.

A VOICE [*singing in the back of the hall*].   Monsieur de Cyrano,
We're tired of tyrannies;
Tyrants have got to go;
So—on with "La Clorise!"

THE AUDIENCE [*echoing*].   "La Clorise!" "La Clorise!"

CYRANO.   Just one more word
Of that cheap song and I will clear the hall!

THE TRADESMAN.   And who are *you*? Samson?

CYRANO.   How did you know?
I'm looking for the jawbone of an ass.
Perhaps you'll lend me yours.

A LADY [*in one of the boxes*].   He goes too far!

A NOBLE.   Shameful!

THE TRADESMAN.   Disgraceful!

A PAGE.   What a lark!

THE AUDIENCE [*divided hisses*].   Ssss! Ssss!
Montfleury! . . . Cyrano! . . .

CYRANO.   Be still!

THE AUDIENCE [*out of control*].   Bow-wow! . . .

Woof! Woof! . . . Kikeriki! . . .
A PAGE.   Miaow! . . .
CYRANO [*louder*].   Once more
    I say be still! [*His voice rises above the tumult, and the shouting
    stops.* CYRANO *goes on in a quieter but no less taunting tone.*]
    I offer one and all
    A general challenge—none will be refused.
    Walk up, you heroes. Give your names. Don't crowd.
    Everyone will be dealt with in his turn.
    Who'll be the first? You, sir? Not you? . . . Then you?
    What! Not you, either? . . . Not even if I send
    The first brave victim straight to glory? Well?
    Won't someone try? Won't someone unafraid
    To die please raise his hand? Not one? Perhaps
    You're all so virginal you'd blush to see
    A naked sword. Refreshing modesty!
    Still—not one name? No upraised hand? Not even
    One little finger? Well, then, I'll resume. [*He turns back to the
    stage, where a miserable* MONTFLEURY *has been tremulously wait-
    ing.*] I aim to have our theatre cleansed or purged
    Of this great boil. And if it can't be cured,
    Then I propose to use—[*He clasps his hand upon his sword.*]
    the scalpel.
MONTFLEURY [*choking*].   I—
CYRANO [*Descends from the chair, places it in the center of the circle, sits
    down, and makes himself comfortable. He then addresses* MONT-
    FLEURY.] O moon, too monstrous and too full—watch me!
    I'll clap my hands three times—like this—and at
    The third handclap you'll disappear.
THE AUDIENCE [*amused*].   Ah! Ah!
CYRANO.   Ready? Here's one!
MONTFLEURY.   I—
A VOICE [*from one of the boxes*].   No!
THE AUDIENCE [*still divided*].   He'll stay! . . . He'll go! . . .
MONTFLEURY.   Gentlemen, I believe—
CYRANO.   Two!
MONTFLEURY.   Really, then,
    Perhaps I should—
CYRANO.   Three!

    [MONTFLEURY *vanishes. A gale of laughter, catcalls and hissing,
    sweeps through the audience.*]

THE AUDIENCE.   Coward! . . . Boo! . . . Come back!

CYRANO [*beams, lolls in his chair, and crosses his legs complacently*].
    Come back? Just let him try.
A CITIZEN.   The manager!

    [BELLEROSE *comes forward, bowing*]

PEOPLE IN THE BOXES.   Ah, Bellerose!
BELLEROSE [*deferentially*].   Choice spirits—nobles all—
THE CROWD IN THE PIT.   Not him! Jodelet, the comedian!
JODELET [*comes forward, speaking through his nose*].   Cattle!
THE CROWD [*laughing*].   Bravo! That's good!
JODELET.   No bravos, please.
    Our friend, the actor with the blossoming bust,
    Was called away—
THE CROWD.   The coward! Boo!
JODELET.   He begs
    For your indulgence. Meanwhile—
THE CROWD.   Call him back! . . .
    No! Let him stay!
THE YOUNG MAN.   Beg pardon, monsieur, but
    Why do you hate Montfleury so?
CYRANO.   Young man,
    There are two reasons, each one great enough
    To earn my condemnation and contempt.
    First: He's a stupid actor, mouths his words,
    Chews up the scenery, and beats the air
    With flailing arms. He leans his weight on lines
    That, otherwise, would soar in singing joy.
    Second: That is my secret.
THE TRADESMAN.   But the play—
    "La Clorise," Baro's masterpiece—must we
    Forego our entertainment for a whim?
CYRANO [*turning his chair to the speaker, and replying respectfully*].
    The poetry of Baro, sir, is worth
    Precisely nothing. Therefore, what I've done
    Is really less than nothing.
LADIES IN THE BOXES.   The idea! . . .
    Our Baro! . . . Really! . . . What a thing to say!
CYRANO [*turns his chair about and addresses the boxes with great gallantry*].   Fair ladies, bloom and brighten. Shine and be
    The center of our dreams. With one slow smile
    Make death a dear delight. Inspire us
    To poetry—but, please, do not attempt
    To judge it.

BELLEROSE.   What about—if I may ask—
  The money to be given back?
CYRANO.   Bellerose,
  That is the first intelligent remark
  I've heard this evening. There should be no holes
  In Thespis' well-worn cloak. So catch this purse—
  And hold your tongue.
  [*He rises and tosses a bag of coins upon the stage.*]
THE AUDIENCE [*dazzled*].   Oh!
BELLEROSE.   At that price, dear sir,
  You've my consent to come and stop "Clorise"
  Each evening in the week.
THE PEOPLE IN THE PIT.   Boo! Boo!
JODELET.   We should be booed as one—
BELLEROSE.   Empty the hall!

  [*As* CYRANO *looks on with obvious satisfaction the audience begins
  to leave. But, overhearing the following conversation, the crowd
  pauses and only a few people go out. The ladies in the boxes have
  risen and put on their cloaks. They, too, stop to listen, and sit down
  again.*]

LE BRET [*to* CYRANO].   Madman!
A BUSYBODY [*coming up to* CYRANO].   Montfleury—it is dangerous.
  The Duke de Candale is his protector.
  Have you a patron?
CYRANO.   No.
THE BUSYBODY.   You haven't one?
CYRANO.   No.
THE BUSYBODY.   Not a friend at court? No powerful lord
  To shield you with the influence of his name?
CYRANO.   I've said it twice. Must I say no three times?
  No, no protector; but—[*He puts his hand on his sword.*]
  a good protectress.
THE BUSYBODY.   But, surely, you'll leave town?
CYRANO.   It all depends.
THE BUSYBODY.   The Duke has a long arm!
CYRANO.   Not quite as long
  As mine, when it is lengthened out—
  [*He displays his sword.*] with this.
THE BUSYBODY.   But, do you dream of daring—?
CYRANO.   Yes. I dream.
THE BUSYBODY.   But—
CYRANO.   On your way!

THE BUSYBODY.   But—

CYRANO.   March! Or tell me why
  You're looking so intently at my nose!

THE BUSYBODY [*confused*].   I—

CYRANO [*coming close to him*].   What's so queer about it?

THE BUSYBODY [*drawing back*].   You mistake—

CYRANO [*pressing still closer*].   You find it flabby, like a swaying trunk?

THE BUSYBODY [*drawing farther back*].   I never—

CYRANO.   Is it crooked, like a beak?

THE BUSYBODY [*still retreating*].   I—

CYRANO.   Does a wart make its tip longer still?

THE BUSYBODY.   But—

CYRANO.   Is a fly taking a promenade
  Upon it? Is it a hideous growth?

THE BUSYBODY.   Oh, no—

CYRANO.   Is it some abnormality?

THE BUSYBODY.   But—I—I've kept my eyes away from it.

CYRANO.   Why have you kept your eyes away?

THE BUSYBODY.   I thought—

CYRANO.   It looks disgusting?

THE BUSYBODY.   Please—

CYRANO.   Its color seems
  Unwholesome?

THE BUSYBODY.   Sir—

CYRANO.   The shape of it's obscene?

THE BUSYBODY.   Certainly not.

CYRANO.   Why the contemptuous look?
  Perhaps you find it just a bit too large?

THE BUSYBODY [*stammering*].   No. On the contrary; it seems quite
  small.

CYRANO.   Small! My nose small! Am I a fool to be
  Ridiculed by an idiot! Small, indeed!

THE BUSYBODY.   Heavens!

CYRANO.   My nose is huge, enormous, vast!
  Listen, poor snub-nose, flat-head, addle-pate,
  Here's an accessory I'm proud to wear;
  For a large nose betokens a large heart.
  Symbol of courage and of courtesy,
  It indicates a nature kind and keen,
  Witty and warm and liberal—like mine—
  And never one like yours, you stupid oaf!
  Because your foolish features are as bare
  Of pride, of passion, and of purity,

Of inspiration, even of a nose—[*He twists* THE BUSYBODY *around
and accompanies the following words with the appropriate action.*]
As that on which I now will plant my boot!

THE BUSYBODY [*running off*].   Help!

CYRANO.   Let this serve as warning to all those
Who find the central portion of my face
A thing for jests. And if the jester is
Well-born, I'll treat him like a noble. He
Will feel my steel instead of leather boots,
And not in back, but front—and higher up!

DE GUICHE [*who, with* THE MARQUISES, *has come down from the stage*].
He's getting tiresome; I'm getting bored.

VALVERT.   He boasts too much.

DE GUICHE.   Will no one stop the man?

VALVERT.   I'll top his wit. I'll match him word for word. [*He swaggers
over to* CYRANO, *who is watching, and assumes a jauntry air.*]
Ahem—your nose—is—very—very—big.

CYRANO [*calmly*].   It is indeed.

VALVERT [*laughs nervously*].   Ha! Ha!

CYRANO.   And is that all?

VALVERT [*perplexed*].   Why, what—

CYRANO.   Too short, young man. You might have said
Many sharp things by varying the tone.
You might have put it some such way as this:
Aggressive: Sir, if I had such a nose
I'd cut it off to please, not spite, my face.
Friendly: A nose like that must dip so deep
A special goblet should be shaped for it.
Descriptive: 'Tis a rock! A peak! A cape!
Did I say "cape"? 'Tis a peninsula!
Inquisitive: Is it an oblong box
For pen and ink? Is it a scissors-case?
Gracious: I see you love the little birds
And offer them this perch for tired feet.
Belligerent: Sir, when you light your pipe,
And smoke blows through your nose, the neighbors cry
"Look out! Another chimney is on fire!"
Kindly: With such a burden on your head,
Take care you do not topple to the ground.
Considerate: Have an umbrella made
To keep its hues from fading in the sun.
Pedantic: Monsieur, Aristophanes'
Hippocamp-elephanto-camelos,

That fabled beast, could not have borne so much
Great bone and heavy flesh upon his head.
Flippant: The latest vogue, I have no doubt;
Clever and fashionable and useful, too:
A perfect hook on which to hang a hat.
Rhetorical: No spiteful wind that blows
Makes you catch cold, O magisterial nose!
Dramatic: When it bleeds, 'tis the Red Sea!
And *what* a sign for a perfumery!
Lyric: Is this the ocean shell, the wreathèd horn,
That Triton blew when the old gods were young.
Innocent: Tell me, when do they unveil
The monument? And may we visit it?
Respectful: My congratulations, sir,
That thing's a house—with a tremendous view!
Rustic: Don't tell me that's a nose. I know
A melon or a giant cucumber
When I see one—and sure I see one now.
Militaristic: Load that gun of yours
And aim it point-blank against cavalry.
Practical: Entered in a lottery
Fifty to one it's sure to take first prize.
Or, in a parody of Pyramus,
Complain and sob: "There is that traitorous nose
Which dared conspire against its master's face
And turned it to a monstrous mockery . . ."
That, my dear sir, is what you *might* have said
Had you the least command of words or wit.
But wit is something you can scarcely spell.
And as for words, you only know the ones
That have three letters, stupid ones like—Ass!
Furthermore, sir, if you had twice the skill
To wage a duel with such pleasantries,
You would have stopped before you could begin
The fumbling first word's stammering syllable.
I laugh at jests like these—when they are mine.
But I permit no other man alive
To utter them.
DE GUICHE [*trying to rescue the gaping* VALVERT].   Come, Valvert.
Come away.
VALVERT [*exploding with rage*].
What arrogance! Airs from a country lout!
A man who—look!—appears in company

In boorish clothes—no gloves—no frills—no lace—
No ribbons—no trim knots upon his sleeves!

CYRANO.   I wear my decorations in my mind.
Clothes make the man, and so I have to be
More careful if less vain. I take great pains
Never to leave my soul uncleansed, nor bear
An insult without washing it away.
I'll not be seen in any company
With conscience dirty and my honor smirched
And every scruple torn to shameful rags.
What shining gems I own, I wear inside.
And when I venture forth, I clothe myself
In independence and sincerity.
Lacking a dashing figure, I contain
My soul as in a corset. I put on
Deeds for my decorations; bristling wit
Instead of perfumed lace and ribbon-knots.
And when I go into the street, the crowd
Will hear the truth ring out like clashing spurs.

VALVERT.   But—

CYRANO.   But I wear no gloves. Alas, you're right.
Too bad. I *did* have one—half of a pair—
But now it's gone. Some fool insulted me;
And so, of course, I flung it in his face.

VALVERT.   Fool! Rascal! Knave! Absurd flat-footed clown.

CYRANO [*takes off his hat and bows, as if* VALVERT *had just introduced
    himself*].   Ah, yes indeed . . . And I am
    Cyrano Savinien Hercule de Bergerac.

VALVERT [*exasperated*].   Buffoon!

CYRANO [*as if seized with cramps*].   Aie! Aie!

VALVERT [*turning back*].   Did you say something more?

CYRANO [*grimacing, as though in pain*].
    It must be exercised. It's getting stiff
    And hurts. It can't be left unused too long.

VALVERT.   What does this mean?

CYRANO.   My sword has gone to sleep
    And tingles to be waked.

VALVERT [*draws his sword*].   So be it then.

CYRANO.   You shall die beautifully.

VALVERT [*contemptuously*].   Poet!

CYRANO.   Yes.
    While swords are clashing, I shall fence in rhyme,
    And improvise a poem, a ballade.

VALVERT.   A ballade?
CYRANO.   Perhaps you may not know the word.
VALVERT.   But—
CYRANO.   A ballade is a peculiar form:
    Three eight-line stanzas built on just three rhymes,
    And each rhyme different—
VALVERT.   This is too much!
CYRANO.   Wait, there's still more. There's the refrain—four lines.
    And at the very last line of the piece
    I'll thrust—and I'll strike home.
VALVERT.   No!
CYRANO.   No, you say? Listen and you will learn:
    "The Duel fought in Hotel Burgundy
    Between a Fool and a De Bergerac."
VALVERT.   And what does all that mean?
CYRANO.   That is the title.
THE AUDIENCE [*wildly excited*].   Quiet!
    Sit down!
    Move over!
    Stop that noise!

[*Tableau. The circle of spectators crowd closer in the pit.* THE
MARQUISES *and officers mingle with the tradesmen. The pages
climb on one another's shoulders to get a better view. All the women
stand up in the boxes.* DE GUICHE *and his aristocratic friends are
on the right. On the left are* LE BRET, RAGUENEAU, CYRANO *and
others.*]

CYRANO [*closing his eyes for a moment*].   Wait! I must choose my
rhymes . . . I have them now.
[*He begins, suiting the action to the words.*]
        My hat is flung swiftly away;
        My cloak is thrown off, if you please;
        And my sword, always eager to play,
        Flies out of the scabbard I seize.
        My sword, I confess, is a tease,
        With a nimble and mischievous brain;
        And it knows, as the blade makes a breeze,
        I shall strike as I end the refrain.

        You should have kept quiet today.
        I could carve you, my friend, by degrees.
        But where? For a start, shall we say
        In the side? Or the narrowest squeeze

'Twixt your ribs, while your arteries freeze,
And my point makes a sly meaning plain?
Guard that paunch! You're beginning to wheeze!
I shall strike as I end the refrain.

I need a word rhyming with "a,"
For, look, you turn paler than cheese
And whiter than—there's the word!—clay.
Your weak thrusts I parry with ease;
Too late now to pause or appease.
Hold on to your spit, though in pain,
For—if you'll permit the reprise—
I shall strike as I end the refrain.

[*He announces with great solemnity:*]

THE REFRAIN

Pray God, prince, to pardon all these
Poor efforts of yours, all in vain.
I thrust [*He thrusts.*] as you sink to your knees;
And I strike—[VALVERT *staggers*; CYRANO *salutes.*]
        as I end the refrain!

[*The hall is in a turmoil. There are shouts from the pit, applause from the boxes. Flowers and handkerchiefs are tossed. The officers surround* CYRANO *and congratulate him.* LE BRET *is both happy and apprehensive.* VALVERT's *friends support him and lead him off stage.*]

THE CROWD [*with one long cry*].   Ahhh!
A GUARDSMAN.   Marvelous!
A WOMAN.   A pretty stroke!
RAGUENEAU.   Superb!
A MARQUIS.   A novelty!
LE BRET.   A madness!
VOICES FROM THE CROWD.   Unexcelled! . . .
        Congratulations! . . . What a feat! . . .
A WOMAN'S VOICE.   The man's a hero!
A MUSKETEER [*approaches and offers his hand to* CYRANO].
        Permit me sir—it was done artfully;
        And I might add I'm something of a judge.
        Not only did I clap my hands, I stamped!
CYRANO [*to* CUIGY].   Who is that gentleman?
CUIGY.   A musketeer.
        His name is D'Artagnan.
LE BRET [*taking* CYRANO's *arm*].   Come, now,

A word with you.

CYRANO. Wait till the rabble goes. [*to* BELLEROSE] May I remain?

BELLEROSE [*respectfully*]. Most certainly.

JODELET [*hearing shouts outside*]. They hoot
And hiss Montfleury.

BELLEROSE [*gravely*]. Ah—"sic transit . . ."
[*to the* DOORKEEPER *and* CANDLE-SNUFFER]
Sweep up. Put out the candles. Close the house.
We'll have our supper; then we shall return
For a rehearsal of tomorrow's play.

[JODELET *and* BELLEROSE *leave, bowing to* CYRANO *as they go.*]

THE DOORKEEPER [*to* CYRANO]. You are not dining?

CYRANO. No. [*The* DOORKEEPER *goes.*]

LE BRET [*to* CYRANO]. Because?

CYRANO [*proudly*]. Because.
[*As soon as the* DOORKEEPER *is out of sight, his tone changes.*]
Because I have no money.

LE BRET [*with the gesture of throwing a bag*]. But that bag
Of clinking coins!

CYRANO. Inheritance—
In one short day it's spent.

LE BRET. How will you live
This month? Or next?

CYRANO. Who knows? Who cares?

LE BRET. What a mad act to throw away your all!

CYRANO. But what a gesture!

THE ORANGE GIRL [*comes from behind her counter and coughs timidly*].
Hem! To see you fast
Affects my heart. Here's everything one needs.
[*She points to the sideboard.*] Take what you like.

CYRANO [*doffing his hat*].
Dear child, although my Gascon pride forbids
Acceptance of one sweetmeat from your hands,
The fear of hurting you outweighs my pride;
So I will take—[*He goes to the sideboard and makes a selection.*]
not much—a grape—[*She presses a whole bunch of grapes upon
him, but he refuses.*] just one.
A glass of water—
[*She tries to pour wine in the glass, but he stops her.*] clear—
and half—just half—
A macaroon. [*He puts back the other half.*]

LE BRET. Folly!

THE ORANGE GIRL.   Oh! Something more!
CYRANO.   One thing. Your hand to kiss.

[*She holds out her hand, and he kisses it as though it were the hand of a princess.*]

THE ORANGE GIRL [*curtsying*].   Thank you. Goodnight.
[*She goes out.*]
CYRANO [*to* LE BRET].   I'll listen now.
[*He stands before the sideboard and puts the macaroon upon it.*]
Dinner! [*Then he places the glass of water in front of him.*]
A drink! [*then the grape*]
Dessert! [*He sits down and starts to eat.*]
Now for the feast! Friend, I was ravenous,
A starving man . . . Oh, you were going to say—
LE BRET.   That all these fools, if you pay heed to them,
Will turn your head. Distrust the treacherous lot.
Take counsel from your friends; men of good sense
Will tell you the effects of insolence.
CYRANO [*finishing his macaroon*].   Terrific.
LE BRET.   And the Cardinal—
CYRANO [*delighted*].   What's that?
The Cardinal was there?
LE BRET [*grimly*].   He must have thought—
CYRANO.   The whole thing quite original.
LE BRET.   But why—
CYRANO.   He is an author—therefore pleased to see
A fellow-author's play jeered off the stage.
LE BRET.   Why do you make so many enemies?
CYRANO [*munching his grape*].   How many would you say I made
tonight?
LE BRET.   Excluding women, I'd say forty-eight.
CYRANO.   Let's count them.
LE BRET.   Montfleury; the tradesman; then
De Guiche; the Viscount; Baro; and the whole
Academy . . .
CYRANO.   Enough. I'm overjoyed.
LE BRET.   And yet this attitude—this way of life—
Where will it take you? What may be your aim?
CYRANO.   For years I wandered in a labyrinth.
There were so many winding ways to choose,
I lost myself. And so I took—
LE BRET.   Which way?
CYRANO.   The very simplest way. I chose the line

Of least resistance. I would be myself—
And please at least myself in everything.
LE BRET [*shrugging*].   So be it. But this hate for Montfleury—
What's the true reason? Can you really tell?
CYRANO [*rising*].   This fat Silenus, who can't reach below
His monstrous belly, this repulsive toad
Still thinks himself a devil with the ladies;
And, while he mouths and waddles through a play,
Casts fishy eyes upon them. I have loathed
The man since first he dared to let his eyes
Rest on her . . . Oh! I thought I saw a slug
Crawling upon a flower!
LE BRET [*astonished*].   What is this?
Can it be possible—?
CYRANO [*with a bitter smile*].   That I should love? [*His tone changes,
and he adds with grave simplicity:*] I love.
LE BRET [*sympathetically*].   I never knew.
You never told me. Will you tell me now?
CYRANO.   With whom I am in love? Reflect, my friend.
This nose which always is ahead of me
By fifteen minutes, scarcely will allow
The dream of being cherished by a frump.
So whom do I adore?—you might have guessed—
Obviously, the fairest of the fair.
LE BRET.   The fairest?
CYRANO.   Yes, the fairest in the world.
The most accomplished, most intelligent, [*despondently*]
In short, the loveliest.
LE BRET.   Who can it be?
CYRANO.   A threat, a peril, though she's unaware
That she can be a danger. Nature's snare;
A damask rose, the perfect trap for love.
Whoever wins her smile wins heaven itself;
Her very gestures show divinity.
Venus was not so lovely in her shell,
Diana never strode the blossoming woods
With half the grace revealed when *she* ascends
Her Sedan chair to ride these Paris streets.
LE BRET.   *Sapristi!* It's quite clear. I understand.
CYRANO.   I knew you'd see.
LE BRET.   Your cousin Madeleine?
CYRANO.   Yes, Roxane. Yes.
LE BRET.   That is good news indeed!

You love her? Tell her so! She watched and saw
You win a rousing triumph here tonight.
CYRANO.   Friend, look at me. Tell me what foolish hope
Remains for me with this protuberance.
No. I have no illusions. Oh, I too
Grow weak and tender in the purple dusk.
A garden calls, and my preposterous nose
Breathes in the April promise. My heart leaps
When, in the light of some enraptured moon,
A woman leans upon her lover's arm.
Thus (so I dream) in such a silver glow,
Would I, too, walk—my arm about my love,
Blissful and blest . . . And then, to cap it all,
I see my profile's shadow on the wall!
LE BRET [*compassionately*].   Dear friend! . . .
CYRANO.   Yes, friend, I have my bitter hours,
Facing this ugliness. When I'm alone,
Sometimes—
LE BRET.   You weep?
CYRANO.   No! That would be too much!
While master of myself, I'll not permit
The soothing beauty of a tear to roll
Along the crooked contours of this nose.
There's a sublimity in tears; and I
Would not debase them; I would never turn
Something sublime to the ridiculous.
LE BRET.   Let's not be gloomy. What is love but chance?
CYRANO [*shaking his head*].   I long for Cleopatra—do I look
Like Caesar?
LE BRET.   But your wit! Your bravery!
The girl who offered you your light repast
Did not find you unbearable.
CYRANO [*reflecting*].   That's true.
LE BRET.   Well, then. As for Roxane—why, she herself
Turned pale during the duel.
CYRANO.   She turned pale?
LE BRET.   Her mind—and heart—already are involved.
Speak to her that she may . . .
CYRANO.   Laugh at my nose?
That is the one and only thing I fear.
THE DOORKEEPER [*enters and presents someone to* CYRANO].
Someone is asking for you, sir.
CYRANO [*startled*].   Good God!

It's her duenna!

THE DUENNA [*with a deep curtsy*].   Someone wants to know
Where her brave cousin may be seen—in secret.

CYRANO [*overwhelmed*].   See me?

THE DUENNA [*with another curtsy*].   See you. Someone would say
something.

CYRANO.   Something?

THE DUENNA [*curtsying again*].   Something.

CYRANO [*staggering*].   Oh, God!

THE DUENNA.   Someone will go
At dawn tomorrow to hear early mass
At Saint-Roch.

CYRANO [*leaning against* LE BRET].   Oh, my God!

THE DUENNA.   Speak fast.

CYRANO.   I must try to think.

THE DUENNA.   Where?

CYRANO.   Where? Let me see—ah, yes. At Ragueneau's,
The pastry-cook's.

THE DUENNA.   Where is it?

CYRANO.   In the Rue—
My God!—Saint Honoré.

THE DUENNA.   Good. She will go.
Be there at seven sharp.

CYRANO.   I will be there. [THE DUENNA *goes out.*]
A rendezvous—from her—with me!

LE BRET.   You see!
Now you are not so miserable, my friend.

CYRANO.   Whatever comes, at least she knows I live.

LE BRET.   And now let's hope you will be calm.

CYRANO [*joyfully*].   Be calm!
I am all frantic violence and fire!
I'd face an army—and I'd vanquish it!
I have ten hearts and twenty arms! I'll fight
With no more dwarfs! [*He shouts wildly.*]
I must have giants now!

[*During the last few minutes, shadows of actors and actresses have been moving about on the stage in the background. They whisper and start the rehearsal. The violinists have come back to their places.*]

A VOICE [*from the stage*].   Silence down there. We are rehearsing.

CYRANO [*laughing*].   Good.
We're going now. [*He goes toward the door—only to be stopped by*

CUIGY, BRISSAILLE, *and several officers who enter supporting*
LIGNIÈRE, *who is very drunk.*]

CUIGY.   Cyrano!

CYRANO.   What is that!

CUIGY.   A heavy song-bird—but without his song.

CYRANO [*recognizing him*].   Lignière! What's happened?

CUIGY.   He's been seeking you.

BRISSAILLE.   He can't go home.

CYRANO.   Why not?

LIGNIÈRE [*in a thick voice, showing a crumpled piece of paper*].
This note warns me—
A hundred lie in wait—because—a song—
Great danger threatens—at the Porte de Nesle—
Must pass there to get home—if I could sleep
At your house—for tonight . . .

CYRANO.   A hundred men
You say? You shall sleep safe in your own house.

LIGNIÈRE [*frightened*].   But—

CYRANO [*in a commanding voice, pointing to the lantern which the*
DOORKEEPER *is swinging*].   Take that lantern. [LIGNIÈRE *seizes it.*]
Start! I swear to you
That I shall tuck you in your bed myself. [*to the officers*]
Come on—but only act as witnesses!

CUIGY.   A hundred men!

CYRANO.   The way I feel tonight
I need them all—I would not have one less!

[THE ACTORS *and* ACTRESSES *in their different costumes have de-
scended from the stage. They listen and come close.*]

LE BRET.   But why involve yourself?

CYRANO.   Le Bret, don't scold.

LE BRET.   And for a worthless sot!

CYRANO.   I'll tell you why:
This reeking sot, this cask of muscatel,
One day did something unforgettable.
Coming from mass, he saw his sweetheart dip
Her fingers in the holy water font.
And this man, who shuns water like the plague,
Went to the basin, bent down over it,
And drank up every drop!

AN ACTRESS [*dressed as a soubrette*].   Ah! That was sweet.

CYRANO.   Yes, was it not?

THE ACTRESS.   But why a hundred men

Against a single poet?

CYRANO.   Let us go! [*to the officers*]

Gentlemen, when you see me charge, keep back.

Withhold your aid, no matter what the odds.

ANOTHER ACTRESS [*jumping down from the stage*].   Oh! I would love
to see this!

CYRANO.   Come along—Come along—

The doctor, Isabel, Leander—all!

You shall compose a proper madcap group,

Quaint actors in a queer Italian farce

Mixed with Spanish drama. You shall be

The jingling bells on this gay tambourine.

ALL THE WOMEN [*joyously excited*].   Bravo! . . . A cape! . . . A cloak! . . .

JODELET.   Come on. Let's go!

CYRANO [*to the Violinists*].   Here, violins, let's march to melody!

[*The violins join in as a line begins to form. Lighted candles are
taken from the footlights and are distributed. It becomes a torchlight
parade.*]

Bravo! First, officers; then, women; then,

Some twenty paces to the front—myself—

[*He takes his position as he speaks.*]

Alone, wearing the plume, the deathless pride

Placed there by Glory . . . Is it understood

No one's to help me? Ready! One, two, three!

Doorkeeper, open the door!

[THE DOORKEEPER *opens the large double doors, and part of old
Paris is seen, suffused in moonlight.*]

Ah! Paris!

The solid city melts away at night

And, underneath the moon, turns into mist,

A magic setting for our little play.

The Seine, like some spellbinding looking-glass

Trembles and glows in this mysterious light.

And now—well, we shall see what we shall see.

ALL.   On to the Porte de Nesle!

CYRANO.   The Porte de Nesle! [*Before he goes, he turns to the* ACTRESS
dressed as a soubrette.]

I think you asked me why a hundred men

Were sent against one poet.

[*He draws his sword and continues calmly.*]

This is why:

This poor, foolhardy poet is my friend.

[*He goes out. A procession follows him—* LIGNIÈRE *staggering along but leading it, then the* ACTRESS *on the arms of the* OFFICERS, *then the* ACTORS *briskly bringing up the rear. As they march to the music of the violins and the flickering flames of the candles, the curtain falls.*]

Act II

The Poets' Cook-shop

THE ROTISSERIE of RAGUENEAU, *chef and pastry-cook. It is actually a large bakery at the corner of Rue Saint Honoré and Rue de l'Arbre-Sec. Through the glass panels of the door there is a broad view of the streets which are still gray, for it is just dawn.*

There is a long counter on the left, with a large iron stand, to which geese, ducks, and white peacocks are fastened. There are china vases with tall bouquets of common flowers, chiefly sunflowers. Farther back is an immense fireplace, in front of which, between great andirons, each one supporting saucepans, various roasts are dripping into the pans.

There is a door to the right. In the rear a staircase leads to a small room, the interior of which is glimpsed through open shutters. In it a table is laid, lit by a small Flemish candelabra. It is a nook which is also a private dining room. A wooden gallery, a continuation of the staircase, leads to similar rooms.

In the center of the shop there is an iron ring, from which large pieces of game are suspended. It is a kind of chandelier and can be let down with a rope.

Under the staircase the ovens cast a red glow. The room is full of copper pots and pans. The spits are turning. Certain foods are piled into pyramids. Hams dangle from hooks. It is the morning's busy hour. Scullions bustle about; tall cooks and undersized apprentices hurry from place to place, their white caps gay with cock's feathers and guinea-hens' wings. Mounds of brioches, cream-puffs, and other pastries are brought in on flat pans and in wicker baskets.

Some of the tables are loaded with food. Other tables are empty, waiting for customers. One table, smaller than the others, is practically hidden under an accumulation of sheets of paper. It is here that RAGUENEAU *is seated, composing. He writes with an inspired air; nevertheless, he keeps ticking off the meter with his fingers.*

FIRST PASTRY COOK [*carrying a fancy confection*].   Nougat with fruits.
SECOND PASTRY COOK [*with another dish*].   Cream custard.
THIRD PASTRY COOK [*bringing a roast decorated with feathers*].   A pea-
cock.
FOURTH COOK [*with a batch of cakes*].   Puff-paste rissoles.
FIFTH COOK [*with a sort of deep-dish pie*].   Filet of beef with juice.
RAGUENEAU [*stops writing and lifts his head*].   The silver smile of
dawn glints on the brass.
Stifle the songs within thee, Ragueneau.
This is the hour for ovens, not for lutes.
[*He rises, and addresses a cook.*]
The sauce needs lenghening; it's much too short.
THE COOK.   How much?
RAGUENEAU.   About three feet.
FIRST PASTRY COOK.   The puff.
SECOND PASTRY COOK.   The pie.
RAGUENEAU [*standing before the fireplace*].   Leave me, my Muse, be-
fore thy limpid eyes
Are reddened by the oven's thickening smoke.
[*He shows a loaf of bread to a* PASTRY COOK.]
You've split your loaves in the wrong place; the pause
Is always in the middle of the line.
[*He shows another* COOK *an unfinished pastry.*]
Add a light roof to this palatial crust.
[*to an* APPRENTICE, *who is putting poultry on a spit*]
And you, my son, should alternate the spit
With a proud turkey and a modest hen,
Just as Malherbe mixed lengthening lines with short;
So turn your roast in strophes in the flames.
ANOTHER APPRENTICE [*coming with a tray covered with a napkin*].
Master! I thought of you and had this baked.
I hope the pattern pleases you. [*He uncovers the tray.*]
RAGUENEAU [*entranced*].   A lyre!
THE APPRENTICE.   Of puff paste!
RAGUENEAU [*moved*].   And with candied fruit!
THE APPRENTICE.   And the strings
Are pure spun sugar.
RAGUENEAU [*giving him a coin*].   Good boy. Drink my health.
[LISE *comes in.*]
My wife. Hush! Hide the money and be off.
[*Uneasily he shows* LISE *the pastry lyre.*]
Is it not fine?
LISE.   It is ridiculous! [*She puts a pile of paper bags on the counter.*]

RAGUENEAU.   Bags? Good. I thank you. [*He looks at them.*]
Lord! My cherished books,
My friends' best poems! Mangled! Torn apart!
Dismembered to make paper bags for pies!
Thus the Bacchantes cut up Orpheus!
LISE [*wryly*].   And have I not the right to use what they,
Your writer-friends, leave for their only pay.
RAGUENEAU.   Ant! Do not scorn the singing grasshopper!
LISE.   Before these scribblers were your bosom friends,
You never called your wife an ant, much less
A wild Bacchante!
RAGUENEAU.   Oh, to do such things
To poetry!
LISE.   It's good for nothing else.
RAGUENEAU.   Then what, I wonder, would you do with prose?

[*Two children come into the shop.*]

Sweethearts, what would you like?
THE FIRST CHILD.   Three patties, please.
RAGUENEAU.   Here they are—nice and brown, and piping hot.
THE SECOND CHILD.   Wrap them up, please.
RAGUENEAU [*aside*].   Alas! One of my bags! [*then, to the children*]
You want them wrapped? [*He picks up a bag and, just as he is
about to put in the patties, he reads:*]
"Ulysses, on the day
He left Penelope . . ." No! Not that one! [*He puts the bag down
and takes another. Before putting in the patties, he reads:*]
"Golden limbed Phoebus . . ." Not that either!
LISE [*impatiently*].   Well!
What are you dallying for?
RAGUENEAU.   There! There!
[*He takes a third bag, with unhappy resignation.*]
"Sonnet to Phyllis . . ." Life is very hard.
LISE.   Luckily he made up his mind, poor fool.

[*She stands on a chair and arranges dishes in a cupboard. Seeing
that her back is turned, RAGUENEAU calls to the children who are already at the door.*]

RAGUENEAU.   Hist, children! Give me back that little bag,
And for the "Sonnet" I will give you six
Patties instead of three.

[*The children give him the bag, snatch the patties, and run off.*

RAGUENEAU *smooths out the paper and begins to read:*]

"Phyllis . . ." A grease spot on that spotless name!
"Phyllis . . ."
CYRANO [*entering abruptly*]. What time is it?
RAGUENEAU [*bowing deeply*]. Just six.
CYRANO [*agitated*]. One hour!
One hour more! [*He walks nervously back and forth.*]
RAGUENEAU [*following him*]. Bravo! I saw—
CYRANO. You mean?
RAGUENEAU. Your victory.
CYRANO. Which one?
RAGUENEAU. The duel at
The Hotel Burgundy.
CYRANO [*deprecatingly*]. Oh, that! The duel—
RAGUENEAU. Fought out in rhyme!
LISE. He talks of nothing else.
CYRANO. Good. But enough of that.
RAGUENEAU. Ah! "I shall strike
As I end the refrain!" How wonderful!
[*He seizes a spit and makes the motions of fencing.*]
"I shall strike as I end the refrain!" [*with mounting enthusiasm*]
"I shall strike—"
CYRANO. What time is it?
RAGUENEAU. Five past six.
"—As I end the refrain!" [*He straightens up.*]
Oh, to compose
A true ballade!
LISE [*to* CYRANO, *who has pressed her hand absent-mindedly passing the
counter*]. What's that? There, on your hand?
CYRANO. Nothing. A little scratch.
LISE. You've been in danger.
CYRANO. Danger? No, not a bit.
LISE [*shaking her finger at him*]. You sound as though
You're telling me a lie.
CYRANO. Did my nose blush
And tremble? Only a tremendous lie
Could do that! [*He changes his tone.*]
I'm expecting someone here.
Unless I wait in vain, leave us alone.
RAGUENEAU. I wish I could; but I expect my poets . . .
LISE [*ironically*]. Prompt for their daily breakfast.
CYRANO. When I give

A sign, get rid of them . . . What time is it?

RAGUENEAU.   Ten after six.

CYRANO [*seats himself nervously at* RAGUENEAU's *table and takes some paper*].   A pen?

RAGUENEAU [*giving him the one behind his ear*].   A poet's quill.

A MUSKETEER [*with a splendid moustache enters and speaks in a stentorian voice*].   Greetings!

[LISE *goes quickly to meet him.*]

CYRANO [*turning around*].   And who is that?

RAGUENEAU.   Friend of my wife.
    A fearless fighter, by his own account.

CYRANO [*takes up the pen and motions* RAGUENEAU *away*].   Hush! [*to himself*] Write. Then fold it. Then give it to her.
    Then run away. [*He throws down the pen.*]
    Coward! But I would die
    Before I dared to speak—[*to* RAGUENEAU]
    What's the time now?

RAGUENEAU.   A quarter past.

CYRANO.   —to speak a single word [*tapping his breast*]
    Of all that's buried here. While if I write . . .
    [*He takes up his pen again.*]
    So I will write the letter I've composed
    More than a hundred times in secret thought.
    Knowing the words by heart, I'll trust my soul
    Readily to recall and copy them.

[*He writes, as thin and hesitant silhouettes move behind the glass door. Shyly, the shadows enter and take on flesh. They are* RAGUENEAU's *protégés, the poets, dressed in black, their stockings awry and spattered with mud.*]

LISE [*entering, to* RAGUENEAU].   Here are your dirty scarecrows—all of them!

FIRST POET [*to* RAGUENEAU].   Brother in art!

SECOND POET [*wringing* RAGUENEAU's *hand*].   Dear colleague!

THIRD POET [*sniffing*].   It smells good
    Here in your eyrie, eagle of pastry-cooks!

FOURTH POET.   Phoebus of chefs!

FIFTH POET.   Apollo of the stove!

RAGUENEAU [*as they surround him, murmuring and embracing*].   How quickly one can feel at home with them.

FIRST POET.   The mob delayed us at the Porte de Nesle.
    Stabbed, soaking in their blood upon the pavement,

Eight cut-throats lay.
CYRANO [*lifting his head*].   Eight? I thought only seven.
[*He goes on with his letter.*]
RAGUENEAU [*to* CYRANO].   I wonder who the hero of such a fight
May be. Perhaps you know him.
CYRANO [*casually*].   I? Not I.
LISE [*to* THE MUSKETEER].   And you?
THE MUSKETEER [*twirling his moustache*].   Perhaps.
CYRANO [*keeps on writing, murmuring a phrase from time to time*].
"I love you—"
FIRST POET.   It's the truth.
One man, they say, beat the entire crowd.
SECOND POET.   It was a fearful sight. The ground was strewn
With sticks and pikes and cudgels.
CYRANO [*writing and murmuring*].   "And your eyes—"
THIRD POET.   And hats were picked up seven streets away.
FIRST POET.   It must have been some terrible—
CYRANO [*still writing*].   "Your lips—"
FIRST POET.   Ferocious giant who performed the deed.
CYRANO.   "And when I see you, I am weak with fear."
SECOND POET [*stealing a cake, to* RAGUENEAU].   Ragueneau, what
new verse?
CYRANO.   —"forever yours." [*He pauses just as he is about to sign his
name, gets up, and puts the letter in his doublet.*]
No need to sign it. I will give it to her.
RAGUENEAU [*replying to the* SECOND POET].   I've made a brand new
recipe in rhyme.
THIRD POET [*seating himself next to a platter of puffs*].   Good! Let us
hear those rhymes.
FOURTH POET [*examining a brioche which he has taken*].
This brioche has
Its cap on crooked. I will straighten it. [*He bites off the top.*]
FIRST POET.   This gingerbread looks at the starving bard
With its sweet almond eyes and such angelic
Eyebrows, made of angelica.
[*He consumes the gingerbread cookie.*]
SECOND POET.   Go on.
We're listening.
THIRD POET [*lightly pressing a round pastry between his fingers*].
This cream-puff bubbles cream,
Smiling at me.
SECOND POET [*nibbling at the pastry lyre*].   For the first time, the lyre
Affords me food.

RAGUENEAU [*coughs, straightens his cap, and assumes the posture of a man about to recite*].

THE RECIPE IN RHYME

SECOND POET [*nudging the* FIRST POET]. Is this your breakfast, friend?
FIRST POET [*to the* SECOND POET].   Is that your dinner?
RAGUENEAU [*declaims*].

ONE OF THE CULINARY ARTS:
HOW TO MAKE FRESH ALMOND TARTS
Break your eggs and beat them whole
    In a bowl.
When they're lighter than a dream
Add some lemon juice like wine,
    And combine
With rich, sweetened almond cream.

Now the puff-paste in the tin
    Is folded in.
Line the mould right to the top,
While your fingers print and pleat
    A pattern neat.
Then you pour in, drop by drop,

The foamy custard in each cup.
    Take them up
Carefully, so nothing parts
From the mixture. Then remove
    To the stove—
And there you have: Fresh Almond Tarts.

THE POETS [*their mouths full*].   Delicious! . . . Exquisite! . . . So tasteful! . . .
ONE OF THE POETS [*choking*].   Humph!

[*They retire, eating, into the background.*]

CYRANO.   Charmed by your voice, see how they stuff themselves.
RAGUENEAU [*softly, with a smile*].   I see. But I won't let them see I see.
    It would disturb me to embarrass them.
    To read my rhymes gives me a double joy:
    I satisfy a weakness of my own,
    And satisfy their weakness—which is food.
CYRANO [*clapping him on the shoulder*].   My friend, I like you.

[RAGUENEAU *joins* THE POETS. CYRANO's *eyes follow him for a moment, then they turn toward* LISE, *who is engaged in a tender conversation with* THE MUSKETEER.]

Lise, does this man,
This doughty warrior, lay siege to you?
LISE [*indignantly*].   One outraged glance of my offended eyes
Would vanquish any suitor rash enough
To doubt my virtue!
CYRANO.   Maybe. But your eyes
Look soft and yielding for a conqueror's.
LISE [*flushing*].   But—
CYRANO [*sharply*].   Ragueneau is my friend, Dame Lise.
I'll see that he's not made a laughing-stock.
LISE.   But—
CYRANO [*raises his voice loud enough to be heard by* THE MUSKETEER].
A word to the wise—take care, my friend.

[*He bows to* THE MUSKETEER *and, after glancing at the clock, goes
to the door and stands there, looking out.*]

LISE [*to* THE MUSKETEER, *who has barely returned* CYRANO'*s bow*].
A gallant lover! Do something! Speak up—
About his nose!
THE MUSKETEER.   About his nose—let's see—
About his nose—[*He moves away from* CYRANO, *followed by* LISE.]
CYRANO [*at the door, motions to* RAGUENEAU *to get rid of his* POETS].
Psst! Psst!
RAGUENEAU [*urging them to the door on the right*].   It's better there—
CYRANO [*impatiently*].   Psst! Hurry!
RAGUENEAU [*pulling them*].   For our poems—
FIRST POET [*with his mouth full*].   But the cakes!
SECOND POET.   Bring them along—we'll scan them there at ease.

[*They follow* RAGUENEAU *after sweeping all the pastry off the trays.*]

CYRANO.   If I detect the first, faint gleam of hope
I will present the letter.

[ROXANE *appears behind the glass door. She is masked and followed by her* DUENNA. *The door is quickly opened by* CYRANO.]

Ah! come in! [*to the* DUENNA]
Two little words with you, Duenna.
THE DUENNA.   Four.
CYRANO.   You like sweet things?
THE DUENNA.   Enough to make me sick.
CYRANO [*swiftly snatches a few bags*].   Here are two sonnets by
Benserade—
THE DUENNA [*disappointed*].   Oh!

CYRANO.   Which I will fill with jelly tartlets.

THE DUENNA [*brightly*].   Ah!

CYRANO.   Are you, perhaps, fond of the cakes called puffs?

THE DUENNA.   Especially when they have cream inside of them.

CYRANO.   I'll bury six of them within the breast
    Of Saint-Amant's new poem. In this ode
    By Chapelain I'll hide a light sponge cake.
    And if you like warm, fresh-baked pies—

THE DUENNA.   Oh, sir,
    I'm mad about them.

CYRANO [*piling the bags in her arms*].   Good. Please take them all.
    Eat them outside. And don't come back until
    The last one's finished.

[*He pushes her out, closes the door, and, removing his hat, goes to
ROXANE. During the ensuing conversation, he remains standing at
a respectful distance.*]

    God bless this moment when you recognize
    My poor existence, and you venture here
    To say . . . to say . . .

ROXANE [*unmasking*].   To thank you first of all.
    That fool, that brainless fop, whom your good sword
    Made fun of, is the one whom a great lord—
    Desiring me—

CYRANO.   De Guiche?

ROXANE [*lowering her eyes*].   —has tried to force
    Upon me—for a husband.

CYRANO.   Ah! I see!
    A substitute? Then I have fought, it seems,
    Not for my ugly nose but your bright eyes.

ROXANE.   Also, I wished . . . But now, before I speak
    And make confession, I must think of you
    Once more as—shall we say—the almost brother
    I used to play with in that lovely park
    Beside the lake.

CYRANO.   I know. You used to come
    To spend your summers down in Bergerac.

ROXANE.   You cut down reeds and said that they were swords.

CYRANO.   You shredded corn-silk for your doll's fair hair.

ROXANE.   Remember the wild berries?

CYRANO.   And the games?

ROXANE.   Those were the days when you did all I asked.

CYRANO.   Roxane—in her short dress—was Madeleine.

ROXANE.   And was I pretty then?

CYRANO.   You were not plain.

ROXANE.   Sometimes when, climbing trees, you cut your hand,
  You'd run to me. And I would act severe
  And, playing mother, I would frown and say:
  "You naughty boy! How did you get that scratch?" [*She takes his
  hand, smiling. Then she stops, surprised.*]
  Too bad! It really is! [CYRANO *tries to withdraw his hand.*]
  And at your age!
  How did it happen to you? When and where?

CYRANO.   Oh, I was playing at the Porte de Nesle.

ROXANE [*seating herself at a table and dipping her handkerchief in a
  glass of water*].   Let's see . . .

CYRANO [*also seating himself*].   Once more the pretty little mother.

ROXANE.   Now tell me all about it, while I wash
  Away this blood. How many did you fight?

CYRANO.   Not quite a hundred.

ROXANE.   Tell me more.

CYRANO.   No more.
  Let's talk of something else. Now *you* tell *me*
  That which you dared not speak of—

ROXANE [*still holding his hand*].   Now I dare.
  The spirit of the past emboldens me.
  Yes, I can tell you now . . . I am in love.

CYRANO.   Ah!

ROXANE.   With a man who does not know it.

CYRANO.   Ah!

ROXANE.   At least not yet.

CYRANO.   Ah!

ROXANE.   But he'll know it soon.
  If he has not suspected it by now.

CYRANO.   Ah!

ROXANE.   Keep your hand there. It seems feverish—
  And yet it trembles on his silent lips.

CYRANO.   Ah!

ROXANE [*tying on a small bandage she has made from her handkerchief*].   And just imagine, cousin, he is in
  Your regiment!

CYRANO.   Ah!

ROXANE [*smiling*].   Yes, he's a cadet
  In your own company!

CYRANO.   Ah!

ROXANE.   On his brow

Genius shines forth. He's witty, noble, proud,
Fearless, and young, and handsome—
CYRANO [*turns pale and gets up suddenly*].   Handsome!
ROXANE.   Yes!
Why, what's the matter?
CYRANO.   Nothing. [*He forces a smile and shows his hand.*]
Just this scratch.
ROXANE.   In short, I love him madly—even though
I've seen him only looking at the play.
CYRANO.   You've never spoken?
ROXANE.   Only with our eyes.
CYRANO.   How do you know that he is—
ROXANE.   People talk.
Under the lindens in the Place Royale
Gossip spreads quickly.
CYRANO.   So he's a Cadet.
ROXANE.   Yes, truly. In the Guards.
CYRANO.   You know his name?
ROXANE.   Baron Christian de Neuvillette.
CYRANO.   Not he.
He is not in the Guards.
ROXANE.   Yes, since today,
With Captain Carbon de Castel-Jaloux.
CYRANO.   How quickly the heart moves! But, my poor child . . .
THE DUENNA [*suddenly opening the glass door*].   Monsieur de
Bergerac, the cakes are gone.
CYRANO.   Then read the verses written on the bags.
[THE DUENNA *disappears.*]
But my poor child, you who love burning words
And flashing wit, what if he is unlearned,
Uncultivated and unpolished, what
If he should be a dolt?
ROXANE.   Impossible!
He wears his hair like one of d'Urfé's heroes.
CYRANO.   His speech may lack the brilliance of his hair.
ROXANE.   I feel—I know—his words will shine and sing!
CYRANO.   What if he has no words? What if he's dull?
ROXANE [*petulantly*].   Then I should die.
CYRANO.   And you have brought me here
To tell me this. It makes but little sense.
ROXANE.   Yesterday, with a sudden shock, I learned
That all the members of your company
Are Gascons—

CYRANO.   And we quarrel with recruits
.   Who, through some favor, get into the ranks
     Of us pure Gascons without being such.
ROXANE.   You can imagine how I fear for him.
CYRANO.   And with good reason.
ROXANE.   Then I thought how strong
     And fine you were—brave and invincible—
     Whipping that lordling, beating off those brutes—
     I thought—I hoped—if you—whom all men fear—
CYRANO.   Enough. I will protect your little baron.
ROXANE.   You will? You promise you'll do this for me?
     I've always felt a tenderness for you.
CYRANO.   I know.
ROXANE.   Then you will be his friend?
CYRANO.   Of course.
ROXANE.   And never let him fight a duel?
CYRANO.   I swear.
ROXANE.   I love you ardently. But I must go.
     [*She replaces her mask and veil, then adds absent-mindedly*]
     Oh, you forgot to tell about the clash
     With all those men. It must have been a sight . . .
     Tell him to write to me at once. [*She blows him a kiss.*]
     You're sweet.
CYRANO.   I will.
ROXANE.   One hundred men against you? . . . So, farewell.
     We're good friends, are we not?
CYRANO.   Of course. Of course.
ROXANE.   Tell him to write . . . A hundred men . . . Be sure
     To tell me all about it later. Now,
     I cannot wait . . . A hundred men . . . How great
     To show such courage!
CYRANO [*bowing*].   I have shown more since.

[ROXANE *goes.* CYRANO *stands motionless, his eyes fixed on the floor. The door on the right is opened and* RAGUENEAU's *head appears.*]

RAGUENEAU.   May we come back?
CYRANO [*still motionless*].   Yes.

[RAGUENEAU *raises his hand and his friends,* THE POETS, *flock in. At that moment* CARBON DE CASTEL-JALOUX, *in his uniform as Captain of the Guard, appears at the glass door in the rear. He greets* CYRANO *with an extravagant gesture.*]

CARBON DE CASTEL-JALOUX.   Ah, look! There he is!

CYRANO [*his head raised*].   Captain!

CARBON DE CASTEL-JALOUX.   Our hero! Yes, we know it all!
   Thirty of my cadets are waiting there.

CYRANO.   But—

CARBON DE CASTEL-JALOUX.   Come along! They wish to honor you.

CYRANO.   No, thanks!

CARBON DE CASTEL-JALOUX.   They're toasting you across the way.

CYRANO.   I can't—

CARBON DE CASTEL-JALOUX [*goes back to the door and shouts in thunderous tones*].   Our hero's disinclined to move.

A VOICE [*outside*].   We'll see to that!
   [*There is a tumultuous sound of clattering boots and swords.*]

CARBON DE CASTEL-JALOUX [*rubbing his hands*].   I thought so! Here
   they come! [THE CADETS *swarm into the shop, with a chorus of
   lusty Gascon oaths.*]

RAGUENEAU [*alarmed*].   Gentlemen, are you *all* from Gascony?

THE CADETS.   All! Everyone!

A CADET [*to* CYRANO].   Bravo!

CYRANO [*bowing*].   Baron!

ANOTHER CADET [*shaking* CYRANO'*s hand*].   Viva!

CYRANO.   Baron!

THIRD CADET [*embracing him*].   I greet you.

CYRANO.   Baron!

SEVERAL CADETS.   Let us all
   Embrace him!

CYRANO [*at a loss*].   Baron! Baron! Baron! Please—!

RAGUENEAU.   And you are also barons, gentlemen?

THE CADETS.   All! Everyone! Our crests and shields piled up
   Would make a formidable tower.

LE BRET [*enters and runs up to* CYRANO].
   They're looking for you everywhere! The mob
   That followed you last night is on your trail!

CYRANO [*apprehensively*].   You did not tell them where I could be
   found.

LE BRET [*gleefully*].   Indeed I did!

A TRADESMAN [*enters, followed by others*].
   Monsieur, the whole Marais
   Is on its way here!

   [*Outside, the street is filled with people, Sedan chairs, and
   coaches.*]

LE BRET [*whispering*].   And Roxane?

CYRANO [*sharply*].   Be still.
THE CROWD [*outside*].   Cyrano! Cyrano! Cyrano!

[*A small mob swarms into the shop, milling about, calling and cheering.*]

RAGUENEAU [*standing on a table and dancing with excitement*].
    They storm into my shop! They break my chairs!
    They ruin everything! It's wonderful.
VARIOUS PEOPLE [*surrounding* CYRANO].   My friend . . . my friend . . .
    my friend . . .
CYRANO.   So many friends—
    So many more than I had yesterday.
LE BRET [*beaming*].   What a success!
A MARQUIS [*coming up with outstretched hands*].   If thou, dear
    friend—
CYRANO.   If "thou"—!
    How did we ever get so intimate?
ANOTHER MARQUIS.   I wish to introduce you to some ladies
    Waiting outside within my carriage.
CYRANO [*coldly*].   Yes?
    And who will introduce you first to me?
LE BRET [*disturbed*].   What's wrong?
CYRANO.   Keep quiet.
A MAN OF LETTERS [*with pen and brief-case*].   May I have details?
    About the—
CYRANO.   No.
LE BRET.   That was Renaudot,
    Editor of the "Gazette."
CYRANO.   Who cares!
A POET [*advancing*].   Sir—
CYRANO.   What! Another!
THE POET.   I intend to make
    An anagram upon your name.
CYRANO.   Enough!

[*The crowd moves and makes way for an obviously important personage. It is the* COUNT DE GUICHE. *He is attended by* CUIGY, BRISSAILLE, *and* THE OFFICERS *who followed* CYRANO *the previous evening.* CUIGY *goes straight up to* CYRANO.]

CUIGY [*to* CYRANO].   Monsieur de Guiche!
    [*The crowd murmurs as* DE GUICHE *comes forward.*]
    He comes here in behalf
    Of Marshal de Gassion—

DE GUICHE [*bowing*]. Who wishes me
    To state his admiration for the feat
    Which has made such a stir.
THE CROWD. Bravo! Bravo!
CYRANO [*bowing*]. The Marshal is a connoisseur of feats.
DE GUICHE. At first he doubted. But these gentlemen
    Swore that they witnessed it.
CUIGY. With our own eyes!
LE BRET [*aside to* CYRANO *who seems abstracted*]. You act as though
    something had hurt you.
CYRANO [*starting*]. Hurt!
    And let the whole world know it! [*He straightens up and throws
    out his chest. His moustache bristles.*]
    You shall see!

    [CUIGY *has been whispering in* DE GUICHE's *ear.*]

DE GUICHE [*nods and speaks:*].
    Your life seems to be full of mighty deeds.
    You serve with these mad Gascons, do you not?
CYRANO. With the Cadets.
A CADET [*with a tremendous voice*]. That's right! He serves with us!
DE GUICHE [*looking at* THE CADETS, *who are now ranged behind*
    CYRANO]. Ah! Can it be these haughty gentlemen
    Are those intrepid warriors . . .
CARBON DE CASTEL-JALOUX. Cyrano!
CYRANO. Yes, captain.
CARBON DE CASTEL-JALOUX.
    Now that the company seems to be complete,
    I'd like you to present it to the Count.
CYRANO [*takes two steps toward* DE GUICHE *and points to* THE CADETS].
      These are Cadets of Gascony,
        Of Carbon de Castel-Jaloux.
      Fighting and lying shamelessly,
      They are Cadets of Gascony.
      They brag of arms and heraldry.
        Their wrath is red, their blood is blue.
      These are Cadets of Gascony,
        Of Carbon de Castel-Jaloux.

      They have storks' legs and eyes as free
        As eagles'; they go storming through
      A crowd with wolf-like savagery.
      They have storks' legs and eyes too free.

They wear their hats haphazardly;
    In spite of plumes, the holes show through.
They have storks' legs and eyes as free
    As eagles'. They go storming through!

Bash-Your-Head and Smash-Your-Knee
    Are nicknames that they've made come true.
Their souls are drunk with ribaldry.
Bash-Your-Head and Smash-Your-Knee:
Wherever a quarrel starts you'll see
    They will be there—and stay there, too!
Bash-Your-Head and Smash-Your-Knee
    Are nicknames that they've made come true.

Ho! You Cadets of Gascony,
    All husbands are fair game for you.
Woman is no divinity
To you, Cadets of Gascony.
Others may weep; you shout with glee!
    Sing taradiddle! And cry cuckoo!
Ho! You Cadets of Gascony!
    All husbands are fair game for you!

DE GUICHE [*dropping casually into an armchair which* RAGUENEAU *has
    hurried to fetch*].   These days a poet is a luxury.
    Nevertheless, would you belong to me?
CYRANO.   No, thank you. Not to anyone.
DE GUICHE.   Last night
    Your rhymes amused my uncle Richelieu.
    I might be of some help to you with him.
LE BRET [*breathless*].   Good Lord!
DE GUICHE.   They tell me you have done five acts
    In rhyme.
LE BRET [*in* CYRANO's *ear*].   You'll get your "Agrippina" played!
DE GUICHE.   Show it to him.
CYRANO [*flattered and tempted*].   Well, really—
DE GUICHE.   He is keen.
    An expert critic, he'll correct the flaws—
CYRANO [*his face darkening*].   Impossible! My blood would turn to ice
    Before I'd take a single comma out.
DE GUICHE.   Then, on the other hand, when he is pleased
    He will pay high for verse.
CYRANO.   Less high than I.
    For when I make a stanza that I like
    I pay for it by singing it myself.

DE GUICHE. You're very proud.

CYRANO. Ah, you have noticed it.

[A CADET *enters with an assortment of hats skewered on his sword. The hats are shabby, full of holes, battered crowns and bedraggled feathers.*]

THE CADET. Cyrano, look! Here is some feathered game.

We caught it on the quay this morning. See—

It is the plumage of the fugitives.

CARBON DE CASTEL-JALOUX. The fruits of victory—[*laughter*]

CUIGY. Whoever paid

That ragged mob must hate himself today.

BRISSAILLE. What scoundrel could have done it?

DE GUICHE. It was I. [*The laughter stops abruptly. In the silence* DE GUICHE *resumes:*]

I hired them to chastise a rowdy fool—

A drunken rhymester—the kind of task

One does not do one's self. [*The silence is profound.*]

THE CADET [*points to the hats and in an undertone, says to* CYRANO:].

What's to be done

With these ripe birds? They'd make a greasy stew.

CYRANO [*takes the sword from him, slides the hats down, and drops them all in one heap at the feet of* DE GUICHE]. Perhaps you will return these to your friends.

DE GUICHE [*rising and speaking brusquely*].

Order my porters and my chair at once! [*to* CYRANO, *angrily*]

And you, sir!

A VOICE [*in the street*]. Porters for the Count de Guiche!

DE GUICHE [*regaining his composure and smiling ironically*]. Have you read "Don Quixote"?

CYRANO. Yes. I take

My hat off to that noble, crackbrained knight.

DE GUICHE. You might re-read the chapter—

A PORTER [*appearing at the door*]. The Count's chair.

DE GUICHE. About the windmills.

CYRANO [*bowing*]. The thirteenth chapter.

DE GUICHE. For when one tilts at windmills, you should know—

CYRANO. Do I fight those who turn with every breeze?

DE GUICHE. That windmills have long arms—arms that can land

You in the mud!

CYRANO. Or lift you to the stars!

[DE GUICHE *leaves. His escort of lords whisper and withdraw.*

LE BRET *accompanies them to the door.* THE CROWD *disperses, but* THE CADETS *remain.* CYRANO *smiles and bows mockingly to those who depart without bowing to him.*]

Gentlemen . . . Gentlemen . . .
LE BRET [*returning and throwing up his hands*].   Oh! What a mess!
CYRANO.   Go on and grumble.
LE BRET.   Leastways you'll admit
Ruining every chance that comes along
Becomes excessive and exaggerated.
CYRANO.   Perhaps I do exaggerate—a little.
LE BRET.   You see!
CYRANO.   But for the sake of principle.
Also in practice I have often found
Exaggeration works extremely well.
LE BRET.   If you would ease that stubborn soul of yours,
If now and then you would forget you were
A musketeer, fortune and fame might come . . .
CYRANO.   What would I have to do? Look for a patron?
Seek some protector and, like clinging ivy,
Crawl round the lordly trunk that holds it up—
Climbing by trickery instead of strength?
No, thank you. Imitate what others do
And dedicate my words to men of wealth?
Become a sedulous ape, a fool who waits
For some official's patronizing smile?
No, thank you. Breakfast every day on toads?
Climb endless stairs? Wear out my knees and back
With bows and bending like an acrobat?
No, thank you. With one hand guard the poor hare
And with the other goad the yelping hounds?
Burn incense for some idol of the hour?
No, thank you. Push, and pull the proper strings?
Become the great man of a little cult?
Trim my frail bark with madrigals for oars
And aging ladies' sighs to fill my sails?
No, thank you. Pay some publisher to print
My verse and bribe some critic to review it?
No, thank you. Get myself elected pope
In wine-shop sessions held by imbeciles?
No, thank you. Get a reputation for
A single sonnet flawless in technique,
Instead of fashioning a hundred others?

No, thank you. Should I be afraid of hacks
And truckle to the worst incompetents?
Say to myself, "Some day, some chance may let
My name appear in the *Mercure François?*"
No, thank you. Should I calculate and scheme,
Plot and grow pale? Make calls instead of rhymes?
Meet the right people, sign the right appeals?
No, thank you. Thank you kindly. No! No! No!
But—I prefer to sing, to dream, to play,
To travel light, to be at liberty,
To look straight, to talk loud and fearlessly,
To cock my hat at any angle; fight
For a quick 'yes' or 'no'—or coin a phrase!
To work without the thought of a reward!
Start on that long-planned voyage to the moon!
Never to write a line that does not ring
With truth, which has its well-spring in the heart.
To be content to say "My garden's small,
My fruits and flowers are few, but they are mine."
Then if success should chance to come my way
No tribute need be paid to Caesar—none.
Whatever fortune—or misfortune—comes
Is mine, and only mine. In short, though I
Am no huge elm or oak-tree, yet I scorn
To be the parasitic ivy. I will climb
Slowly, uncertainly, and so perhaps
To no great height. But I will climb alone.

LE BRET.   Alone, so be it. But not pledged to turn
Against the world! Where did you ever get
This mania for making enemies?

CYRANO.   From seeing you make friendships easily
With people whom you flatter—and despise.
I force myself to make a few faint friends;
But I am overjoyed when I can say:
"I made another enemy today!"

LE BRET.   This is sheer lunacy!

CYRANO.   And my pet vice.
Being unpleasant gives me curious pleasure.
The pulse pounds with excitement when you march
Beneath a battery of hostile eyes!
You wear your doublet with a prouder air
When it is stained with someone's envious gall.
Those softening friendships comforting and warm,

Are like the high Italian collars, lace
Which decorates the neck and weakens it;
For, though you feel at ease, there's no support,
The neck bends right and left—and the head's turned.
Whereas for me, hate is a stiffening ruff.
Its rigid starch holds the neck proudly high,
And each new enemy's another pleat.
Hatred's a Spanish collar, hard and tight;
It frames you like a vice—or like a halo.
LE BRET [*He is silent for a moment. Then he puts his arm around*
    CYRANO.].
    Go on, be bitter. Face the world with scorn.
    But tell me secretly she loves you not.
CYRANO [*vehemently*].   Be still, I tell you!

    [CHRISTIAN *enters and attempts to mingle with the other* CADETS,
    who do not notice him. Finally he sits down alone, and LISE *comes
    up to wait on him.*]

A CADET [*seated at a table in the back, raises his glass to* CYRANO].
    Hi, there! Cyrano!
    Let's have the story.
CYRANO.   In a little while. [*He walks to the back with* LE BRET *and
    they converse quietly at the rear.*]
THE CADET [*rising*].   The story of the fight—ah, that will teach
    [*He stops in front of* CHRISTIAN.]
    This timid young recruit a thing or two.
CHRISTIAN [*raising his head*].   Timid recruit?
ANOTHER CADET.   Yes, weakling from the north.
CHRISTIAN.   Weakling?
FIRST CADET [*tauntingly*].   Monsieur de Neuvillette, know this:
    There is one subject that is never mentioned.
    It is like saying "rope" in the same house
    In which someone was hanged.
CHRISTIAN.   And what is that?
ANOTHER CADET [*in portentous tones*].   Look—look at me! [*With an
    air of mystery he taps one finger three times against his nose.*]
    Now do you understand?
CHRISTIAN.   You mean his—
ANOTHER CADET.   Hush! That word is never spoken. [*He points to
    CYRANO, who is still talking backstage with* LE BRET.]
    Unless you want to settle things with him!
ANOTHER CADET [*insinuatingly*].
    He killed two hulking men because they snuffled

And angered him by talking through their noses.
ANOTHER CADET [*in a hollow voice*].
    One reference to that fatal cartilage—
    You'll die before your time.
ANOTHER CADET [*putting his hand on* CHRISTIAN's *shoulder*].
    Just say one word—!
    Did I say "word"? A single careless look!
    If you take out your handkerchief, you might
    As well take out your burial cloth.

[*All* THE CADETS *stand around* CHRISTIAN *with folded arms. He rises and crosses over to* CARBON DE CASTEL-JALOUX, *who is talking to an* OFFICER.]

CHRISTIAN.   Captain!
CARBON DE CASTEL-JALOUX [*turning and examining* CHRISTIAN *from head to foot*].   Monsieur?
CHRISTIAN.   What can one do when Southerners grow boastful?
CARBON DE CASTEL-JALOUX.
    Show them that, though a man comes from the North,
    Courage comes with him. [*He turns away.*]
CHRISTIAN.   Thank you.
FIRST CADET [*calling to* CYRANO].   Now for the story.
ALL THE CADETS.   The story!
CYRANO [*coming forward*].   Oh—my story?

[THE CADETS *draw up chairs and benches and lean forward.* CHRISTIAN *sits astride a chair.*]

Well, I went
Alone to meet them. In the sky, the moon
Shone like the great white watch, when suddenly
The heavenly watchmaker began to draw
A wad of cotton clouds about the face
Of this bright time-piece, and the night became
The darkest night the world had known. The quays
Were evil holes of blackness. You could see
No further than—
CHRISTIAN.   Your nose?

[*The silence is tremendous. Everyone is startled and rises.* THE CADETS *turn to* CYRANO, *who has stopped abruptly.*]

CYRANO.   Who is that man?
A CADET [*in a low voice*].   A raw recruit who came to us this morning.
CYRANO [*scrutinizing* CHRISTIAN].   This morning?

CARBON DE CASTEL-JALOUX.   Baron Christian de Neuvill—

CYRANO [*checking himself*].   Very well. [*He turns white, then red, and
    seems about to hurl himself upon* CHRISTIAN.]
    I—! [*He controls himself with a great effort and resumes in a
    strained voice.*]
    As I was saying—[*Then with a burst of rage*]
    God! [*Again he recovers himself and continues.*]
    Well, as I said, the night was dark. [*General astonishment.* THE
    CADETS *take their seats again and watch* CYRANO *tensely.*]
    I walked,
    Thinking that for a shabby ne'er-do-well
    I would offend some prince, some mighty lord,
    Who might well have me taken—

CHRISTIAN.   By the nose.

CYRANO [*in a choked voice*].   Taken into custody; pull out my teeth;
    In short, I was perhaps unwise to poke—

CHRISTIAN.   Your nose—

CYRANO.   My fingers in the crack between
    The bark and the tree-trunk. This person might
    Rap me upon—

CHRISTIAN.   Your nose.

CYRANO [*mopping perspiration from his brows*].   Upon my knuckles.
    But I said, "Duty calls! Gascon, march on!
    Go forward, Cyrano!" When, from the dark,
    I felt a blow—

CHRISTIAN.   Upon your nose.

CYRANO.   I sprang
    And swiftly parried it. I found myself—

CHRISTIAN.   Nose against nose.

CYRANO [*leaping at him*].   Almighty God in heaven!

    [*All* THE CADETS *expect murder, but, reaching* CHRISTIAN, CYRANO
    again masters himself and goes on:]

    I found myself pitted against a hundred
    Cut-throats who stank—

CHRISTIAN.   To make you hold your nose.

CYRANO [*pales, but smiles coldly*].
    Who stank of onions and sour wine. I rushed,
    Head down—

CHRISTIAN.   Nosing the scent.

CYRANO.   Head down, and charged!
    I ran through two, ripped one, and gored another.
    Then someone countered—Paf!—and I went—

CHRISTIAN. Pif!
CYRANO [*bursting all bonds*]. Out! Heaven help you! Out! The lot of
  you!

  [THE CADETS *rush toward the doors.*]

FIRST CADET. At last the tiger's roused!
CYRANO. I warn you—out!
  And leave this man alone with me!
SECOND CADET. Poor chap.
  We'll find him ground to mince-meat.
RAGUENEAU. Mince-meat?
ANOTHER CADET. Yes.
  In one of your meat-pies!
RAGUENEAU. I'm turning pale
  And limp as any napkin.
CARBON DE CASTEL-JALOUX. Let us go.
FIRST CADET. He'll carve him into tidbits.
SECOND CADET. I'm afraid
  To think of what will happen.
ANOTHER CADET [*shutting the door as the last* CADET *leaves*]. It will be
  Something too terrible to think about.

  [THE CADETS *have left—through the doors up the stairs.* CYRANO
  and CHRISTIAN *stand face to face.*]

CYRANO. Embrace me!
CHRISTIAN. Sir—
CYRANO. You're brave.
CHRISTIAN. Oh! but—
CYRANO. Yes, brave.
  I like you.
CHRISTIAN. But I feel—
CYRANO. I say embrace me.
  I am her brother.
CHRISTIAN. Whose?
CYRANO. Why, hers, of course!
CHRISTIAN. What!
CYRANO. Yes, Roxane's.
CHRISTIAN [*rushing toward him*]. Heavens! You are her brother!
CYRANO. Well, *almost.* I am her brotherly cousin.
CHRISTIAN. And she has told you—?
CYRANO. All.
CHRISTIAN. And she loves me?
CYRANO. Perhaps. Well—probably.

CHRISTIAN [*impulsively grasping his hands*].   You'll never know
      How very much your friendship means to me.
CYRANO.   Isn't the friendship just a trifle sudden?
CHRISTIAN.   Forgive me—
CYRANO [*looking at him, with one hand on his shoulder*].   True
      enough, the rogue *is* handsome.
CHRISTIAN.   I wish I could express my admiration!
CYRANO.   But all those noses—
CHRISTIAN.   Let me take them back!
CYRANO.   Roxane expects a letter—
CHRISTIAN.   Then I'm lost.
CYRANO.   And why?
CHRISTIAN.   Because—and I could kill myself
      For shame—I am a fool, a stupid fool.
CYRANO.   No man's a fool who calls himself a fool.
      And your attack on me was scarcely stupid.
CHRISTIAN.   Oh that! Words always fly when one attacks;
      I have a soldier's glib supply of speech.
      But women tie my tongue; they strike me dumb.
      Their eyes are full of kindness when I pass—
CYRANO.   And hearts are even kinder when you stop?
CHRISTIAN.   No, they are not. For I am one of those
      Who cannot talk of love. I tremble and I feel—
      But words refuse to come.
CYRANO.   Whereas I think
      Had Nature only shaped me differently
      I could have talked of love—and talked—and talked!
CHRISTIAN.   Oh, to express one's thoughts with wit and grace!
CYRANO.   To be a musketeer with a smooth face!
CHRISTIAN.   Roxane's an intellectual. I know
      She'll see through me at once.
CYRANO [*looking at him*].   Oh, if I had
      Such an interpreter who could translate
      The language of my heart!
CHRISTIAN [*despondently*].   I must have words!
      Beautiful words!
CYRANO [*suddenly*].   And you shall have them! Yes,
      I'll lend them to you! You shall lend your looks,
      Your winning features and all-conquering charm,
      And we will make—between the two of us—
      One paragon, one hero of romance!
CHRISTIAN.   What do you mean?
CYRANO.   Would it be hard to learn

To say the things I'd teach you day by day?
CHRISTIAN. What?
CYRANO. Your Roxane shall not be disillusioned.
　　If you will let my soul speak through your lips,
　　Together we shall woo—and win her, too.
CHRISTIAN. But, Cyrano, do you propose—?
CYRANO. Christian,
　　Are you afraid?
CHRISTIAN. I am. You frighten me.
CYRANO. Alone, you fear to make her heart turn cold.
　　If you will put my phrases on your tongue
　　You'll see how soon we set her heart on fire!
CHRISTIAN. Your eyes are burning!
CYRANO. Well—what do you say?
CHRISTIAN. And would it give you so much pleasure?
CYRANO [*carried away*]. Yes! [*He stops himself suddenly, and his enthusiasm drops to an impersonal tone.*]
　　Yes, it might be amusing. It would be
　　The very sort of thing to tempt a poet.
　　I'll be your other self and you'll be mine;
　　We will complete each other. You'll go on
　　To certain victory, and I will be
　　The shadow at your side. You'll represent
　　My absent beauty and I'll be your wit.
CHRISTIAN. But, wait! That letter I'm supposed to write!
　　I never could achieve—
CYRANO [*taking out the letter which he had written*]. Here is your letter.
　　Everything is there, except the signature.
CHRISTIAN. I can't—
CYRANO. You can. You must. Be reassured.
　　It's a good letter.
CHRISTIAN. But—you had it ready?
CYRANO. We poets always have a stock on hand
　　Of odes and tender tributes to some fair,
　　Imagined Chloris. A fond fantasy.
　　A dream blown in the bubble of a name.
　　Exchange that dream for truth;
　　Turn the vague fiction into breathless fact;
　　And all my fancies flitting aimlessly
　　Will come to earth and perch about her heart.
　　My letter is an artist's tour de force—
　　Most eloquent where it is least sincere.
　　Take it—and let me hear no more about it.

CHRISTIAN.   Will many of the words have to be changed?
   Written haphazard, will it fit Roxane?
CYRANO.   Take my word, it will fit her like a glove!
CHRISTIAN.   But—
CYRANO.   Love—or self-love—is so credulous
   Roxane will be convinced that she inspired
   Each breathing, brilliant word.
CHRISTIAN.   My friend! My friend!

   [*He throws himself into* CYRANO'*s arms. They remain locked in an
   embrace as* A CADET *cautiously opens a door and puts his head in.*]

THE CADET.   No sound. The solid silence of the grave.
   I am afraid to look. [*He looks.*]
   What's this!

   [*The others enter and see* CYRANO *and* CHRISTIAN *rapturously embracing.*]

   Ah! . . . Oh! . . .
A CADET.   Really, this is too much!

   [*General consternation*]

THE MUSKETEER.   Now we shall see.
CARBON DE CASTEL-JALOUX.   And has our sinner turned into a saint?
   When he is badly smitten on one nostril
   Does he present the other?
THE MUSKETEER.   It seems safe
   To speak about his nose.
   [*He calls to* LISE *with an air of approaching triumph.*]
   Here, Lise! Watch this!
   [*He makes a point of sniffing the air with great ostentation.*]
   Now this is most surprising! What a stench!
   [*He approaches* CYRANO.]
   Surely you must have noticed how it smells
   Of—what is it?
CYRANO [*slaps his face and sends him sprawling*].   A bursting bag of
   wind!

   [THE CADETS *rejoice, finding their* CYRANO *unchanged. They
   shout, leap and turn somersaults as the curtain falls.*]

Act III

Roxane's Kiss

A LITTLE *square in the old Marais. The houses are ancient and there is a view of old and narrow streets. On the right is* ROXANE'S *house with an ivy-hung garden wall and thick foliage above it. There is a jasmine-festooned balcony with a large window above the door. There is a stone bench, and rough stones project from the wall. By the use of these, it is easy to climb to the balcony. The balcony window is wide open.*

On the left, directly opposite ROXANE'S *house, is an old mansion of similar style, brick and stone, with an entrance door. The door's metal knocker is wrapped in linen, like the bandage of a bruised thumb.*

As the curtain rises the DUENNA *is seated on the stone bench. Near her stands* RAGUENEAU, *dressed in a kind of livery. He is finishing a story and wiping his eyes.*

RAGUENEAU.   And then she vanished—with this musketeer!
　　　Alone and ruined—what was I to do?
　　　Well, so I hanged myself. I breathed my last,
　　　When our Monsieur de Bergerac came in.
　　　Cutting me down, he offered me the post
　　　Of steward to his cousin. Here I am.
THE DUENNA.   But how did all this ruin come about?
RAGUENEAU.   Lise adores all soldiers; I love poets.
　　　The cakes Apollo left were seized by Mars.
　　　You can see how the story had to end.
THE DUENNA [*rising and calling to the open window*].   Roxane, they're
　　　waiting. Are you coming soon?
ROXANE'S VOICE.   I'm putting on my cloak.
THE DUENNA [*calling* RAGUENEAU's *attention to the house opposite*].
　　　They've gathered there,
　　　At Clomire's house—a salon for the wits.
　　　This afternoon a paper will be read
　　　Upon "The Tender Passion."

RAGUENEAU.   "The Tender Passion"?
THE DUENNA [*with a sigh*].   Ah, yes! [*She calls again.*]
Roxane, you must come down at once
Or we shall miss the lovely discourse on
"The Tender Passion."
ROXANE'S VOICE.   I am coming now.

[*There is a sound of stringed instruments coming nearer.*]

CYRANO'S VOICE.   La! la! la! la!
THE DUENNA [*flustered*].   Is it a serenade?
CYRANO [*followed by two* PAGES *playing on lutes*].
I tell you it's a demi-semi-quaver,
You demi-semi-fool!
FIRST PAGE [*ironically*].   Of course you know
A demi-semi-quaver, sir?
CYRANO.   Of course.
Like all the pupils of Gassendi, I
Am a prepared musician.
THE PAGE [*singing and playing*].   La! la! la!
CYRANO [*snatching the lute and completing the musical phrase*].   La!
la—I'll take the melody—la! la!
ROXANE [*appearing on the balcony*].   Oh! It is you!
CYRANO [*continuing the air*].   I come to serenade
Your lilies and salute your roses too.
ROXANE.   I'm coming down.
THE DUENNA [*pointing to* THE PAGES].   Where did you find those
master virtuosi?
CYRANO.   I won them from D'Assoucy. We discussed
A point in grammar. "Yes!" and "No!" it raged
When suddenly I saw these raw-boned gawks,
Scraping away—he takes them always with him.
I said "Let's bet a day of music." "Done,"
Said he—and lost. So, till the sun rolls round,
I have these lutanists tied to my heels,
Melodious witnesses of all I do.
At first it was delightful; then less so;
And now it bores me. [*He turns to the two* PAGES.]
Leave me. Run away.
Play a depressed pavane for Montfleury. [THE PAGES *go toward the
back of the stage.* CYRANO *turns to* THE DUENNA.]
I come, as I do every night, to ask
Roxane . . . [*He calls to* THE PAGES *as they are leaving.*]
Play a long time—and out of tune!

[*Then he speaks again to* THE DUENNA.]
　　To ask if he, her soul and heart's elected,
　　Is still perfection, faultless as he is fair?
ROXANE [*emerging from the house*].
　　He is. How wonderful! How full of wit!
　　And how I love him!
CYRANO [*smiling*].　Christian, then, is witty?
ROXANE.　Ah yes, dear cousin, even wittier
　　Than you.
CYRANO.　It makes me happy to admit it.
ROXANE.　No one alive can say such pretty things,
　　So dexterously, so delicately, as he.
　　Sometimes, perhaps, his Muse is at a loss;
　　His fancy falters. And then, suddenly,
　　He utters phrases, airy, wingèd words—
　　Those little nothings which mean everything.
CYRANO.　Indeed!
ROXANE.　Cousin, I do not like your tone.
　　It's sharp and skeptical—just like a man.
　　Because a person has a handsome face
　　You say—or you imply—he is a fool.
CYRANO.　And so he talks with skill and subtlety.
ROXANE.　Talks? He does more than merely talk. He teaches!
CYRANO.　And does he write?
ROXANE.　Still better. Listen to this:
　　"The more you take away my heart, the more
　　You leave to me." [*She looks at* CYRANO *triumphantly.*]
　　What do you think of that!
CYRANO.　Pooh!
ROXANE.　And he writes in verse as well as prose.
　　[*She declaims the lines.*]
　　"Since hearts were made to join and not to part,
　　If you steal mine, send me your own, dear heart."
CYRANO.　At first he has too much, then not enough.
　　Just how much heart will keep him satisfied?
ROXANE.　Your teasing is too rough; your jealousy—
CYRANO [*startled*].　My what!
ROXANE.　You're jealous of another poet,
　　One who can write with piercing tenderness:
　　"Believe me, my poor heart has but one cry,
　　One note of longing that can never die.
　　And if my silent kisses could be penned,
　　You'd read my letter with your lips, sweet friend."

CYRANO [*smiling with satisfaction in spite of himself*].　Good! Very
　　good! Those lines are— [*He stops himself and finishes with pa-
　　tronizing disdain.*]
　　Well, they sound
　　Terribly affected.
ROXANE.　Indeed? And this—
CYRANO [*happily*].　You quote his letters? Know them all by heart?
ROXANE.　Every last one.
CYRANO.　That's surely flattering.
ROXANE.　He is a master!
CYRANO [*deprecatingly*].　Oh—a master?
ROXANE [*peremptorily*].　Yes!
CYRANO.　So be it. He's a master.
THE DUENNA [*who has been discreetly in the rear, comes forward*].
　　Monsieur de Guiche! [*She urges* CYRANO *toward the house.*]
　　He should not find you here.
　　Go in. He might suspect . . . might even guess—
ROXANE.　My secret! He is powerful; he thinks
　　He is in love with me—and if he knew
　　My heart, he'd have us all in ruins!
CYRANO.　Well . . .

　　[*He enters the house just before* DE GUICHE *appears.*]

ROXANE [*making a curtsy to* DE GUICHE].　I was just going out.
DE GUICHE.　I came to say
　　Farewell.
ROXANE.　Where are you going?
DE GUICHE.　To the war.
ROXANE.　Ah!
DE GUICHE.　Yes. Tonight.
ROXANE.　Ah!
DE GUICHE.　Orders have arrived.
　　We will lay siege to Arras.
ROXANE.　Ah! A siege!
DE GUICHE.　You take my going rather coolly.
ROXANE.　Oh!
DE GUICHE.　This grieves me. Shall we ever meet again?
　　And when? And do you know I have been made
　　Commander of the entire camp?
ROXANE [*with complete indifference*].　Bravo!
DE GUICHE.　The regiment of the Guards—
ROXANE [*startled*].　The Guards?
DE GUICHE.　The one

In which your cousin, that loud boaster, serves.
I shall revenge myself on him out there.
ROXANE [*gasping*].   The Guards are going?
DE GUICHE [*smiling*].   It's my regiment.
ROXANE [*aside, sinking to the bench*].   Christian!
DE GUICHE.   Is anything the matter?
ROXANE [*with emotion*].   Yes. This departure—strikes me to the heart—
 To know that he—the one I care for most—
 Is on his way to war!
DE GUICHE [*with pleased surprise*].   For the first time,
 And on the very day of my departure,
 You have a kind and tender word for me.
ROXANE [*changing her tone as she fans herself*].   Would you revenge
 yourself upon my cousin?
DE GUICHE.   But you are on his side.
ROXANE.   Oh, on the contrary.
 I am against him.
DE GUICHE.   Yet you see him—
ROXANE.   Seldom.
DE GUICHE.   One meets him everywhere—in company
 With one of the Cadets—with—what's his name—
 Neuvillen—Neuviller—
ROXANE.   A tall man?
DE GUICHE.   Blond.
ROXANE.   Red-headed.
DE GUICHE.   Rather handsome.
ROXANE.   Pooh!
DE GUICHE.   And dumb!
ROXANE.   He looks it . . . But regarding Cyrano:
 You think, perhaps, the way to punish him
 Is to expose him, place him in the thick
 Of battle? That's the very thing he'd love!
 I know a better way to break his pride.
DE GUICHE.   And that is?
ROXANE.   When the regiment departs,
 Leave him and his Cadets, his boon companions,
 Right here in Paris. Here, with folded arms,
 Make them sit out the war. And let him rage!
DE GUICHE.   O woman! Woman! No one but a woman
 Could dream of such a sly and subtle trick!
ROXANE.   He'll eat his heart out, and his angry friends
 Will gnaw their nails for being left behind.
 They'll cry and curse—and you will be avenged.

DE GUICHE [*coming closer*].   You love me, then, a little?
[*She forces a smile.*] Can I hope
That being on my side's a sign of love?
ROXANE.   It is a sign.
DE GUICHE [*showing her several sealed documents*].   Here are the
marching orders.
They will be sent to all the troops—except
[*He detaches one envelope.*]
This one—for the Cadets. [*He puts it in his pocket.*]
This one I'll keep . . .
So much for Cyrano's great lust for battle! . . .
And it is you who outwit people—you!
ROXANE.   Sometimes.
DE GUICHE [*close to her*].   You drive me mad. Listen. Tonight—
I should be going with the troops—but how,
Feeling that you are kind, can I depart!
Listen. Not far off, in the Rue d'Orléans,
There is a convent of the Capuchins.
A layman dare not enter—but I know
The Fathers—things can be arranged.
Their sleeves are wide and I could hide in them.
They wait upon my uncle Richelieu
As household priests who tend his private chapel.
Fearing the uncle they'll protect the nephew.
Others will think me gone . . . I will come masked.
Give me one day, dear lady of caprice.
ROXANE.   But, should it come to light, your glory—
DE GUICHE.   Bah!
ROXANE.   And there's the siege of Arras—
DE GUICHE.   Let it wait!
It will be none the worse. But let me stay!
ROXANE [*tenderly*].   Alas!
I should forbid it.
DE GUICHE.   Ah!
ROXANE.   No—you must go. [*Aside*]
Christian stays here. [*Aloud*]
I know that you will be
A shining hero—Antoine!
DE GUICHE.   You pronounce
The name and make it new. You like it, then?
ROXANE.   It makes me tremble.
DE GUICHE [*enraptured*].   Good! Now I can go. [*He kisses her hand.*]
Are you content?

ROXANE. Ah, yes indeed! Ah, yes,
My friend!

[DE GUICHE *goes out.*]

THE DUENNA [*who has been in the background, comes forward and makes a mock curtsy behind* DE GUICHE's *back*]. Ah, yes, my friend.

ROXANE [*to* THE DUENNA]. Don't breathe a word
To Cyrano. He'd never pardon me
For robbing him of his belovèd war. [*She calls toward the house.*]
Cousin! We're going over to Clomire's.
[*She points to the opposite house.*]
Alcandre is to speak—and Lysimon.

THE DUENNA [*putting her little finger in her ear*]. My little finger says we shall not hear them.

CYRANO [*emerging, as* ROXANE *and* THE DUENNA *reach the door*]. Oh, never miss those educated monkeys.

THE DUENNA. Look! There's a linen cloth around the knocker!
[*She addresses it.*]
So, noisy one, they've gagged your brassy tongue,
Lest you compete with longer orators!
[*She knocks cautiously and quietly.*]

ROXANE [*seeing the door open*]. Let us go in.
[*She pauses on the threshold to address* CYRANO.]
If Christian comes today,
As I feel sure he will, ask him to stay.

CYRANO [*suddenly, just as* ROXANE *is disappearing into the house*].
And what, according to your other talks,
Will be the subject of your conversation?

ROXANE. I'll ask about—

CYRANO [*quickly*]. About—?

ROXANE. You'll keep it quiet?

CYRANO. Quieter than a wall.

ROXANE. Well—about nothing!
I'll merely say: "Begin! Let yourself go!
Talk about love! Be brilliant! Improvise!"

CYRANO [*smiling grimly*]. Good!

ROXANE. Sssh!

CYRANO. Sssh!

ROXANE. Remember! Not a word! [*She enters and the door shuts.*]

CYRANO [*bowing*]. A thousand thanks!

[*The door opens again, and* ROXANE *puts out her head.*]

ROXANE.   He must not be prepared!
CYRANO.   Certainly not!
BOTH [*together*].   Sssh! Sssh!

[*The door closes.*]

CYRANO.   Christian! Come here! [CHRISTIAN *enters.*]
    I've found out all we need to know. Prepare
    Your choicest thoughts! There's little time to lose!
    Don't look so woebegone! This is your chance
    For victory! . . . Come to your house with me,
    And I will teach you—
CHRISTIAN.   No!
CYRANO.   What's that?
CHRISTIAN.   I'll wait
    For Roxane here.
CYRANO.   What's happened to you? Come,
    You must learn quickly—
CHRISTIAN.   No. I've learned enough.
    I'm tired of borrowed words and fancy phrases;
    Of acting out a part, trembling with fear,
    At first it was a novelty. But now
    I know she loves me; I am not afraid.
    I'll speak up for myself.
CYRANO.   You will?
CHRISTIAN.   I will.
    What makes you think I don't know how to talk?
    Am I so stupid? Well, then, you shall see!
    It's true, my friend, I've learned a lot from you,
    But instinct tells a man what he should say—
    And how to take a woman in his arms!
    [*He sees* ROXANE *leaving* CLOMIRE's *house.*]
    It's Roxane! Cyrano! Don't leave me now!
CYRANO [*bowing to him*].   Now is the time, my friend. Speak for your-
    self.

[*He disappears behind the garden wall as* ROXANE *comes out of* CLOMIRE's *house with others. She takes leave of her friends, curtsying to them.*]

ROXANE.   Barthénoïde . . . Alcandre . . . Grémoine . . .
THE DUENNA [*disappointed*].   We missed the discourse on "The Tender Passion." [*She goes into* ROXANE's *house.*]
ROXANE [*curtsying again*].   Urimédonte . . . Farewell . . .

[*The departing friends curtsy to* ROXANE, *to each other, and sepa-rate. They go down different streets.* ROXANE *sees* CHRISTIAN.]

Oh! It is you! [*She goes toward him.*]
The night is falling. Wait. They have all gone.
The air is sweet. No one comes by. Sit here.
Speak to me. I am listening.

[CHRISTIAN *sits next to her on the bench. There is a deep silence. At last* CHRISTIAN *speaks.*]

CHRISTIAN.   I love you.
ROXANE [*closing her eyes*].   Ah! Speak to me of love!
CHRISTIAN.   I love thee.
ROXANE.   That is the theme. Go on. Embellish it.
CHRISTIAN.   I love—
ROXANE.   Embellish it!
CHRISTIAN.   —Love you so much!
ROXANE.   Obviously. And then? . . . And then?
CHRISTIAN.   And then—I would be happy if—if you—
    Loved me. Roxane, say that you love me, too.
ROXANE [*pouting*].   You give me gruel—I expected sweets!
    Explain the way you love!
CHRISTIAN.   Why—very much.
ROXANE.   Oh! Disentwine your knotted sentiments!
CHRISTIAN.   Your neck—I long to kiss it!
ROXANE.   Christian!
CHRISTIAN.   I love thee!
ROXANE [*rising to go*].   What! Again!
CHRISTIAN [*detaining her*].   I love thee not!
ROXANE [*reseating herself*].   That's promising.
CHRISTIAN.   For I adore thee!
ROXANE [*getting up and moving away*].   Oh!
CHRISTIAN.   I'm growing dull.
ROXANE.   And that distresses me
    As much as though you had grown old and ugly.
CHRISTIAN.   But—
ROXANE.   Follow and find your vanished eloquence.
CHRISTIAN.   But I—
ROXANE [*goes toward the house*].   I know. You love me. So farewell.
CHRISTIAN.   Not yet! I tell you—
ROXANE [*opening the door*].   That you adore me.
    Yes, yes. I know. Goodbye. And go away.
CHRISTIAN.   But I—

[ROXANE *shuts the door in his face.*]

CYRANO [*who has entered without being seen or heard*].   Bravo! It was
    a great success!
CHRISTIAN [*desperately*].   Help me!
CYRANO.   Not I!
CHRISTIAN.   But I shall die unless
    I win her favor—and immediately.
CYRANO.   And how the devil can I tell you what
    To do—immediately.
CHRISTIAN [*seizing his arm*].   Ssh! There she is!

    [*The balcony window is lit up.*]

CYRANO [*moved*].   Her window!
CHRISTIAN.   I shall die!
CYRANO.   Lower your voice.
CHRISTIAN [*whispering*].   Shall die.
CYRANO.   The night is dark—
CHRISTIAN.   What then?
CYRANO.   Something
    May still be salvaged, though you don't deserve it.
    Stand there, poor fool, facing the balcony.
    I'll stay beneath, prompting the words for you.
CHRISTIAN.   But—
CYRANO.   Hold your tongue!
THE PAGES [*appearing in the background*].   Hollo there!
CYRANO.   Stop that noise!
FIRST PAGE [*in a low voice*].   We've played the sad pavane for Mont-
    fleury.
CYRANO [*in an equally low voice, hurriedly*].
    Then lie in wait and watch. One at this corner;
    And one at that. If someone passes by,
    Strike up a tune.
SECOND PAGE.   What sort of tune, O pupil of Gassendi?
CYRANO.   Gay for a woman; gloomy for a man.
    [THE PAGES *go, one to each street corner.* CYRANO *turns to*
    CHRISTIAN.] Call her!
CHRISTIAN.   Roxane!

    [CYRANO *picks up a few pebbles and throws them against the window.*]

CYRANO [*to* CHRISTIAN].   Wait till she answers this.
ROXANE [*opening the window a trifle*].   Who calls me?
CHRISTIAN.   I!

ROXANE. And who is "I"?

CHRISTIAN. Christian.

ROXANE [*scornfully*]. Oh, you!

CHRISTIAN. I want to speak to you.

CYRANO [*under the balcony*]. That's good.
Keep your voice low.

ROXANE. No. I have heard enough.
Your speech is stupid. Go away.

CHRISTIAN. Forgive—

ROXANE. No longer do you love me.

CHRISTIAN [*repeating* CYRANO'*s whispered words*]. What a charge!
No longer love you!—when—by all the Gods!—
I love you more and more!

ROXANE [*starts to close the window but stops*]. A trifle better.

CHRISTIAN [*following* CYRANO'*s prompting*].
Yes, more and more. Love grows—rocked in my heart,
Which, cruelly, the little wanton babe
Takes for his cradle.

ROXANE [*coming forward on the balcony*]. Better still . . . But if
This love is cruel why not stifle it
Before it leaves the cradle?

CHRISTIAN [*as before*]. I have tried—
But—madam—all in vain. This infant is—
A new-born Hercules.

ROXANE. Ah! You improve!

CHRISTIAN. So that he strangled—with his little fists—
That pair of deadly serpents—Pride and—Doubt.

ROXANE [*resting her arms on the balcony rail*].
Ah! That is good! But why so hesitant?
You stumble. Has your active mind gone lame?

CYRANO [*drawing* CHRISTIAN *under the balcony and, in the darkness, slipping into his place*]. Wait! This becomes too difficult!

ROXANE. Tonight
Your words are halting. Why is that?

CYRANO [*speaking low like* CHRISTIAN]. Because
The time is night. Groping around in darkness
They must move slowly till they find your ear.

ROXANE. But mine have no such trouble.

CYRANO. This is why:
Yours find their way into my heart at once.
My heart is large—your ears are very small.
Besides, your words descend while mine must climb;
Descent is swift, but to surmount takes time.

ROXANE.   Yet, in the last few moments, they have learned
    To make the trip more quickly.
CYRANO.   Exercise
    Strengthens their wings—and now they know the way.
ROXANE.   And am I speaking from so great a height?
CYRANO.   So great that you would kill me instantly
    If one hard word were dropped upon my heart.
ROXANE [*moving*].   Now I am coming down.
CYRANO [*quickly*].   No! No!
ROXANE.   Then climb.
    Mount by the stone bench there. Come quickly!
CYRANO [*alarmed, drawing back into the darkness*].   No.
ROXANE.   Why not?
CYRANO [*with ever-increasing emotion*].
    Let me enjoy this precious mood
    Of magic. Let us speak unfettered and
    Unseen.
ROXANE.   But why unseen?
CYRANO.   It's witchery.
    Everything is half hidden, half revealed.
    You sense the blackness of a trailing cloak;
    I feel the whiteness of a summer gown.
    I am a shadow—you a gleam of light.
    This is what these mad moments mean to me . . .
    If ever I were eloquent—
ROXANE.   You were! You are!
CYRANO.   But never have the words run from my heart
    With such real passion.
ROXANE.   Why?
CYRANO.   Because—till now—
    I spoke uncertainly. A dizzy haze
    Clouded my vision. But tonight it seems
    I speak for the first time of love—to you.
ROXANE.   It's true your voice sounds different tonight.
CYRANO [*fervently*].   Yes, it is different. In the sheltering dark
    I dare to be myself at last. I dare—[*He stops in complete confusion.*]
    Where was I?—What have I said?—I could not guess—
    This force, so fascinating—and so new . . .
ROXANE.   So new?
CYRANO [*floundering, trying to recapture the mood*].   So new to be sin-
    cere. So new
    Not to give way to fear of being mocked.
ROXANE.   For what?

CYRANO.   For my absurd and reckless dreams.
　　　My heart puts on a masquerade of wit.
　　　I aim to bring a star down from the sky—
　　　And stoop, in shame, to pluck a common flower.
ROXANE.   A common flower has charm.
CYRANO.   But not tonight.
　　　Tonight I want the star!
ROXANE.   Before tonight
　　　You never spoke with such free eloquence.
CYRANO.   Tonight I scorn to use love's rhetoric—
　　　Its quivers, arrows, torches, amorous darts!
　　　I need a language that is fresh and pure.
　　　Instead of sipping little thimblefuls
　　　Of sugared water, I would slake my thirst
　　　At the wide river when it is in flood.
ROXANE.   Ah, but your wit?
CYRANO.   It was a mere technique.
　　　I used it to attract you. But tonight—
　　　Here in this artless world, this perfumed hour—
　　　Wit has no place. The glittering words
　　　That garnish letters trimmed with hearts and flowers
　　　Would be an insult. With a single star
　　　Heaven rebukes all frantic artifice.
　　　I fear that, in our skillful alchemy,
　　　True sentiment may be too subtilized
　　　And vanish in a smoke—and we will have
　　　For our poor soul's refined finality
　　　Only the last refinement of the fine.
ROXANE.   But wit—?
CYRANO.   Is hateful when it plays with love.
　　　It turns frank passion into foolish fencing.
　　　Besides, the moment comes—and pity those
　　　For whom it never comes—when love resents
　　　Clever ripostes and nimble repartee,
　　　Instead of what is deeply felt and nobly told.
ROXANE.   And if that moment has arrived—is here
　　　For both of us—what words would you employ?
CYRANO.   All words, all thoughts, all natural flowers of speech!
　　　I'd throw them all together as they come—
　　　Not in a carefully arranged bouquet.
　　　I love you—and I suffocate with love.
　　　I love you—I am mad—It is too much!
　　　Your name is like a bell hung in my heart;

And every time I think of you, Roxane,
I tremble and the swinging bell rings out!
Nothing about you is forgot, for I
Love every little memory of you.
One day last year—it was the twelfth of May—
You changed the way you wore your hair. Your hair
Was like the radiant light of day to me—
I was like one who dared to look upon
The mid-day sun. So, after you passed by,
All things my eyes could see were washed with gold.

ROXANE [*agitated*].   Yes, this is love.

CYRANO.   And nothing else but love,
Jealous and terrible and sad,
And yet not selfish. I would sacrifice
My happiness for yours without a twinge,
Though you should never know about the gift,
If I might hear, far off as in a dream,
A little of the laughter I had brought.
Each look from you lifts and ennobles me—
A virtue I had never felt before.
Now do you begin to understand?
Now do you feel my soul climb through the dark?
Truly, it is too beautiful, too rare:
This hour—this desperate avowal—and you,
Listening in the night! It is too much!
Even in my proudest, most importunate dreams,
I never hoped for this! Nothing is left
But to die now, die at the topmost peak! . . .
Have words of mine the power to make you tremble?
For you are trembling in the blue-black branches,
A trembling leaf among the shaken leaves.
I feel the tender quivering of your hand
Descend along the pulsing jasmine vine.
[*He passionately kisses the end of a dangling spray.*]

ROXANE.   Yes, I am trembling. I am weeping, too.
And I am yours. I love you utterly.
Drunk—madly drunk—with love.

CYRANO.   Then let death come,
For it is I who brought about this madness.
I ask for nothing . . . Yes, for one thing more.

CHRISTIAN [*beneath the balcony*].   A kiss!

ROXANE [*drawing back a little*].   What?

CYRANO.   Oh!

ROXANE.   You asked for—?

CYRANO.   Yes, I asked—[*whispering to* CHRISTIAN]
   You go too fast.

CHRISTIAN.   This is no time to stop.
   Let's take advantage of the tender mood.

CYRANO [*to* ROXANE].   I asked—it's true I asked—but now I know
   My brusque demand was too presumptuous.

ROXANE [*obviously chagrined*].   I see. You don't insist upon it now.

CYRANO.   Well, I insist—without insisting. Yes,
   I know your maidenly reserve is shocked.
   And so this kiss—well, grant it not.

CHRISTIAN [*tugging* CYRANO'S *cloak*].   Why not?

CYRANO.   Be silent, Christian! Hush!

ROXANE [*leaning over*].   What did you say?

CYRANO.   I hushed myself for having gone too far.
   I said, "Be silent, Christian!" [*The sound of lutes is heard.*]
   Wait! I hear
   Someone approaching.

[ROXANE *closes her window.* CYRANO *listens to the music: one lute plays a gay tune; the other plays a melancholy melody.*]

Now what may this mean?
A sad tune mingled with a merry one.
A man—and yet a woman . . . Ah, a monk!

[A CAPUCHIN *monk enters carrying a lantern. He goes from house to house, peering at the doors.* CYRANO *comes forward to intercept him.*]

Whom do you seek, O new Diogenes?

THE MONK.   I'm looking for the house . . .

CHRISTIAN [*whispering impatiently to* CYRANO].   Get rid of him!
   He's in the way!

THE MONK.   Of Madeleine Robin . . .

CHRISTIAN.   What does he want?

CYRANO [*pointing to a street in the background*].
   That way—keep to the right—
   Then straight ahead.

THE MONK.   Tonight I'll tell—and thanks—
   My rosary for you to the last bead.

CYRANO.   Good luck to you. And blessings on your cowl.

[*He goes back to* CHRISTIAN, *who takes* CYRANO *by the arm.*]

CHRISTIAN.   Get me that kiss!

CYRANO.   No.
CHRISTIAN.   Now or later—
CYRANO.   True.
>   It must occur—that agony of delight
>   When your two trembling mouths are bound to meet
>   Because of your moustache and her red lips. [*to himself*]
>   I'd like it better if it were because—

[*The shutters open and, at the sound,* CHRISTIAN *retreats. He hides beneath the balcony as* ROXANE *comes out and leans on the balcony railing.*]

ROXANE.   Are you still there? You spoke about—about—
CYRANO.   A kiss. The word is sweet. Why should your lips
>   Fear to pronounce it? If it burns them now,
>   What will it do when words turn into deeds?
>   Do not be frightened. Even now I felt
>   How you stopped teasing and passed fearlessly
>   From smiles to sighs, and then from sighs to tears.
>   Oh, pass once more, slowly, unconsciously—
>   From tear to kiss is but a quick heart's beat.
ROXANE.   Ah, hush!
CYRANO.   A kiss, when all is said, is—what?
>   A compact sealed, a promise carried out.
>   An oath accomplished and a vow confirmed.
>   The rosy dot upon the "i" in "loving."
>   A secret for no ear, but for the lips.
>   The velvet humming of an amorous bee:
>   The endless moment of infinity.
>   The heart's communion cup that tastes of flowers.
>   The breathing in of a little of the soul
>   When the pure spirit rises to the lips.
ROXANE.   Ah, hush!
CYRANO.   A kiss has such nobility
>   That even the queen of France—the queen herself—
>   Bestowed a kiss upon a favored lord.
ROXANE.   And so?
CYRANO [*with mounting passion*].   And so, like Buckingham, the lord,
>   I've suffered and been still. Like him I love
>   My queen unswervingly. Like him I am
>   Faithful and sad . . .
ROXANE.   And, like him, you are fair;
>   Yes, handsomer than Buckingham.
CYRANO [*his ardor suddenly quenched*].   Alas!

I had forgotten just how fair I was.

ROXANE. Then climb and take this bud that blooms for you.

CYRANO [*pulling* CHRISTIAN *toward the balcony*]. Climb up!

ROXANE [*murmuring*]. This cup that tastes of flowers . . .

CYRANO. Climb!

ROXANE. This velvet humming of a bee . . .

CYRANO [*impatiently*]. Climb! Climb!

CHRISTIAN [*hesitating*]. I am afraid—is this the proper time?

ROXANE. This moment of infinity . . .

CYRANO. You fool!

Climb now! At once!

[*He pushes* CHRISTIAN, *who springs forward, and, after mounting the bench and climbing up the vines, reaches the balcony, jumps over the railing, and takes* ROXANE *in his arms.*]

CHRISTIAN. Roxane! Ah, my Roxane!

CYRANO. There's a strange hunger gnawing at my heart—
This lingering kiss, this sumptuous feast of love,
Where I am Lazarus . . . Yet, in the dark,
There falls a crumb or two to comfort me.
For on another's lips I feel her kiss,
Kissing the passionate words I spoke—my words! [*The lutes are heard again.*]
The sad tune—the gay air . . . Once more the monk!
[CYRANO *runs across the stage, pretending to have come from a considerable distance. He cries out in a clear voice:*]
Halloa!

ROXANE. Who is it?

CYRANO. I. I came this way—
Is Christian still about?

CHRISTIAN [*surprised*]. What! Cyrano!

ROXANE. Good evening, cousin.

CYRANO. Truly, a good evening.

ROXANE. I'm coming down.

[*She disappears into the house as* THE CAPUCHIN MONK *comes down the street.*]

CHRISTIAN [*seeing him*]. Oh! He again! [*He follows* ROXANE.]

THE MONK. It's here—
I'm sure it is—Madeleine Robin—here.

CYRANO. I thought you said Ro-*lin*.

THE MONK. I said Ro-*bin*.
B, i, n, *bin*!

[ROXANE *appears on the threshold, followed by* CHRISTIAN *and*
RAGUENEAU *carrying a lantern.*]

ROXANE.   What is it?
THE MONK.   I have a letter.
CHRISTIAN.   A what?
THE MONK.   It must be something spiritual,
    Some holy message—sent by a great lord.
ROXANE [*to* CHRISTIAN].   It's from de Guiche.
CHRISTIAN.   He dares!
ROXANE.   But not for long.
    I love you—he has ceased to trouble me. [*She breaks the seal of the
    letter and, by the light of* RAGUENEAU's *lantern, reads it to herself.*]
    "Mademoiselle: The drummers beat their drums;
    My men are putting on their uniforms;
    They think that I have gone. But I am here—
    Here at the convent. Having disobeyed you,
    I plan to visit you, and send you word
    By one—a poor lamb of a monk—who knows
    Nothing of this . . . Your lips smiled tenderly;
    Your eyes looked kind. I cannot go until
    I see them once again—familiarly.
    Therefore, dismiss your servants. Be alone,
    And graciously receive a suitor who
    Though too audacious, is, he dares to hope,
    Already pardoned. One who signs himself,
    Etcetera . . . etcetera . . ." [*to* THE MONK]
    Listen. This is the way the letter reads. [*All gather around her, as
    she pretends to read the message.*]
    "Mademoiselle: The Cardinal's desire
    Must be obeyed, however difficult.
    Therefore I send these lines by a discreet,
    Most reverend and holy Capuchin.
    It is our wish—our will—that you permit
    This friar to perform the ceremony
    Of marriage in your home, this night, at once. [*She turns the page.*]
    Secretly, then, you must become the bride
    Of Christian, who is being sent to you.
    I know you would not choose him. Be resigned.
    Heaven will recompense you. Be assured
    Once more of the respect of one who is,
    And will be ever—yours, etcetera . . ."
THE MONK [*beaming*].   The noble lord! I said so—did I not?

I knew it had to do with something sacred.

ROXANE [*whispering to* CHRISTIAN].   How do you like my way of reading letters?

CHRISTIAN.   Hmm!

ROXANE [*aloud*].   But this is terrible—!

THE MONK [*directing the light toward* CYRANO].   You are the man?

CHRISTIAN.   No. It is I.

THE MONK [*turning the lantern toward* CHRISTIAN, *puzzled when he
sees* CHRISTIAN's *obviously handsome features*].   But—

ROXANE [*hastily*].   Look! Here is a postscript!
"Be sure to give the worthy Capuchin
One hundred and twenty pistoles for the convent."

THE MONK.   The noble, noble lord!
[*to* ROXANE] So be resigned.

ROXANE [*with a martyred air*].   I am resigned.

[RAGUENEAU *opens the door for* THE MONK. CHRISTIAN *ushers him
in, while* ROXANE *pauses to whisper to* CYRANO.]

De Guiche will soon be here.
Keep him engaged—somehow. Don't let him in
Until—

CYRANO.   I understand.
[*to the* MONK] How long to tie
This nuptial knot?

THE MONK.   A quarter of an hour.

CYRANO.   Go in. I will wait here.

[ROXANE *and* CHRISTIAN *enter the house. The door closes.*]

How to detain
De Guiche for fifteen minutes . . .
[*He leaps to the bench and begins to mount the wall.*]
Let us climb.
I think I have a plan.
[*The lutes are heard again. This time the tune is definitely sad.*]
It is a man.   [*The tremolo becomes more intense and melancholy.*]
This time it is a man indeed!
[CYRANO *reaches the balcony. He pulls his hat over his eyes, re-
moves his sword, wraps his cloak about him, and looks down.*]
Up high.
But not too high.
[*He crosses the balcony and, finding a long branch, takes hold of it
with both hands, ready to let himself drop to the ground.*]
Alas, I must disturb

This so serene, salubrious atmosphere.

[DE GUICHE *enters. He is masked and feels his way uncertainly in the darkness.*]

DE GUICHE. What can that idiot Capuchin have done?
CYRANO [*to himself*]. Careful! He must not recognize my voice . . .
I will assume the native Gascon tone.
DE GUICHE [*peering at the house*]. This must be it. I cannot see too well.
The mask annoys me . . . Still, this is the house . . .
[*He starts to enter the house. Just before he reaches the door,* CYRANO, *holding on to the branch, jumps from the balcony. He lands between* DE GUICHE *and the door and pretends to have dropped from a great height. He lies motionless on the ground, as though stunned. Startled,* DE GUICHE *leaps back.*]
What's this? [*He raises his eyes, but the branch has sprung back and, seeing nothing but the sky, he is bewildered.*]
Where did this thing—this man—fall from?
CYRANO [*sitting up, and speaking in a broad Gascon accent*]. The moon.
DE GUICHE. What! From the moon!
CYRANO [*seemingly half-awake*]. What time is it?
DE GUICHE. He's lost his mind. Nevertheless . . .
CYRANO. What time? What day? What country? Where am I?
DE GUICHE. But, sir—
CYRANO. I am confused
DE GUICHE. But, sir—
CYRANO. I fell
Straight from the moon, like a great bomb!
DE GUICHE [*exasperatedly*]. Oh, come!
CYRANO [*rising, angrily*]. I tell you from the moon!
DE GUICHE [*placatingly*]. Good . . . Good . . . You fell
Out of the moon . . . [*Aside*] The man is raving mad.
CYRANO [*coming close to him*]. It was not metaphorical, that fall!
DE GUICHE. But—
CYRANO. Did it take a hundred years? Or more?
Or one swift moment? I have no idea.
How long was it—I have lost track of time—
Since I explored that saffron-colored globe?
DE GUICHE [*shrugging*]. I don't know. Let me pass.
CYRANO [*blocking him*]. But where am I?
Be frank with me. Hide nothing. In what place,
On what spot have I fallen from the sky?

DE GUICHE.   Good God!
CYRANO.   I could not choose my landing place—
    The fall was much too fast. So tell me now
    Where my disbalanced weight has hurtled me.
    Is this some other moon? Another world?
DE GUICHE.   I tell you, sir, I must—

[CYRANO *suddenly cries out in terror.* DE GUICHE *is alarmed and draws back.*]

CYRANO.   My God! I'm in a savage country where
    Men have black faces!
DE GUICHE [*putting his hand to his face*].   What!
CYRANO [*with a show of fear*].   Am I, perhaps,
    In darkest Africa? Are you a native?
DE GUICHE [*remembering his mask*].   This mask!
CYRANO [*pretending to be reassured*].   Aha! Then I must be in Venice!
DE GUICHE [*again trying to pass*].   A lady waits—
CYRANO [*completely assured*].   Oh! Then I am in Paris!
DE GUICHE [*smiling in spite of himself*].   The fellow is amusing.
CYRANO.   Ah! You laugh!
DE GUICHE.   I laugh—but want to pass.
CYRANO [*happily*].   So I have fallen
    Right into Paris! [*He is now perfectly at ease. He brushes himself, bows, and, beaming at* DE GUICHE, *goes on:*]
    You must pardon me—
    I came by the last cloudburst; there is ether
    All over me. My eyes are full of star-dust.
    There's fur from some strange planet on my spurs.
    And—look!—here on my cuff, a comet's hair!
    [*He puffs out his lips as if to blow it away.*]
DE GUICHE [*beside himself*].   Enough!
    [*He tries again to pass, but* CYRANO *intercepts him, stretching out a leg as if to show him something.*]
CYRANO.   And here—deep in my calf—there is
    A tooth from the Great Bear. Trying to miss
    A prong of Neptune's trident, I sat down
    Deep in the Scales, which registered my weight
    In heaven forever. [*He prevents* DE GUICHE *from leaving by taking hold of a button on* DE GUICHE's *doublet.*]
    Should you press my nose
    Milk would spurt out!
DE GUICHE.   Milk!
CYRANO.   From the Milky Way!

DE GUICHE.   By Hell itself!

CYRANO.   Oh, no! By heaven I came. [*He folds his arms.*]
> You never would believe the things I saw.
> You'd never guess that Sirius wears a night-cap. [*confidentially*]
> The Little Bear is still too small to bite. [*laughing*]
> As I went through the Lyre I snapped a string. [*proudly*]
> I'm going to write a book about it all;
> And every little golden star I caught
> At great risk in my scorching cloak, shall serve
> As asterisks.

DE GUICHE.   No more of this! I wish—

CYRANO.   I know what you are driving at!

DE GUICHE.   Monsieur!

CYRANO.   You'd like to learn the way the moon is made
> And just what sort of creatures live in it.

DE GUICHE.   No, no! I want—

CYRANO.   To know how I achieved
> The perilous voyage there. I used a means
> Entirely my own.

DE GUICHE [*hopelessly*].   The man is mad.

CYRANO [*scornfully*].   I did not use the stupid eagle of
> Regiomontanus or that other bird,
> The dove of Archytas.

DE GUICHE [*muttering*].   A lunatic—
> But still, a learned one.

CYRANO.   I did not do
> Anything which a man had done before.
> [DE GUICHE *manages to slip by and goes toward* ROXANE's *door.*
> CYRANO *follows him, ready to hold him by force, if necessary.*]
> I have discovered six astounding means—
> Six ways to violate the virgin air.

DE GUICHE [*turning, interested*].   Six, did you say?

CYRANO [*persuasively voluble*].   First, I anoint my body,
> Stark naked, with the heavens' morning tears
> Captured in crystal vials. Then I lie
> Stretched out in light, and let the sun's full blaze
> Draw me to heaven as it draws the dew.

DE GUICHE [*fascinated, taking a step toward* CYRANO].   Yes, that is one.

CYRANO [*drawing him away from the door*].   Then there's the second way:
> I can condense a powerful rush of wind
> By rarefying air within a chest,
> Using a twenty-sided burning-glass.

DE GUICHE [*taking another step*].   That's two.

CYRANO [*drawing him still further away*].   Or, since I have some man-
   ual skill,
   Make a mechanical grasshopper.
   I feed his springs of steel with gunpowder,
   And, with successive blasts of fire, I mount
   Into the upper pasture of the stars.
DE GUICHE [*following him and counting on his fingers*].   Three.
CYRANO.   And since smoke is bound to rise, I blow
   Enough into a globe to carry me
   High up above the world.
DE GUICHE.   And that makes four.
CYRANO.   Diana, goddess of the moon, draws a long bow;
   But when her bow is slender, she sucks out
   Marrow from oxen. So I smear myself
   With it, and wait to be sucked skyward.
DE GUICHE [*still following*].   Five. [*While talking,* CYRANO *has drawn*
   DE GUICHE *to the other side of the square, near a stone seat.*]
CYRANO.   Lastly, I sit upon an iron plate.
   And fling a magnet high into the air.
   The iron flies to join the magnet. Then
   I throw the magnet further off . . . And so
   I can ascend this way indefinitely.
DE GUICHE.   Six. Six good ways. And which one did you choose?
CYRANO.   A seventh.
DE GUICHE.   A seventh method? What was that?
CYRANO.   You'd never guess.
DE GUICHE.   The rascal interests me.
CYRANO [*making the sound of waves accompanied by large mysterious
   gestures*].   Hoouih! Hoouih!
DE GUICHE.   Well?
CYRANO.   Can't you guess it?
DE GUICHE.   No.
CYRANO.   The tides! When the full moon tugged at the sea,
   I soaked myself and waited on the sand,
   Dripping with brine, especially my hair;
   For hair retains the water in its mesh.
   Then the moon pulled. I rose—I rose straight up.
   Swift as an angel—gently—without strain . . .
   And then I felt a shock. And then . . .
DE GUICHE [*sinking on the seat, overcome by curiosity*].   And then? . . .
CYRANO [*resuming his natural voice*].   And then . . . a quarter of an
   hour has passed.
   A marriage has been made—and you are free.

DE GUICHE [*springing up*].   What's this? Can I be drunk! I know that
   voice!

   [ROXANE's *door opens and lackeys appear carrying a lighted candelabra.* CYRANO *removes his hat.*]

   I know that nose, too! Cyrano!
CYRANO [*bowing*].   The same.
   This is the moment. They've exchanged the rings.
DE GUICHE.   Who? [*He turns and sees, behind the lackeys,* ROXANE
   and CHRISTIAN *hand in hand.* THE CAPUCHIN MONK *follows, smil-
   ing, also* RAGUENEAU, *with a candlestick.* THE DUENNA, *showing
   evidences of a hasty toilet, clad in a wrapper, brings up the rear.*]
   Good Lord!
   [*to* ROXANE] You! [*recognizing* CHRISTIAN *with astonishment*]
   And he! [*bowing to* ROXANE *with grudging admiration*]
   A clever trick. [*to* CYRANO]
   My compliments, O maestro of machines.
   Your story would have held at Peter's gate
   A famished saint hungry for Paradise.
   Do not forget the details, they would make
   A lively book.
CYRANO [*bowing*].   Thank you for the advice.
   I hope to follow it.
THE MONK [*to* DE GUICHE, *indicating the lovers with great satisfaction*].
   My son, a charming couple, thanks to you.
DE GUICHE [*coldly*].   Indeed. [*to* ROXANE]
   Madame, be good enough to say
   A farewell to your husband.
ROXANE.   What?
DE GUICHE [*to* CHRISTIAN].   The troops
   Are on their way. Join them.
ROXANE.   To go to war?
DE GUICHE.   Of course.
ROXANE.   But the Cadets—they are not going!
DE GUICHE.   They will go. [*He takes a paper from his pocket.*]
   Here's the order. [*to* CHRISTIAN] Take it, baron;
   Deliver it at once.
ROXANE [*throwing herself into* CHRISTIAN's *arms*].   Christian! Christian!
DE GUICHE [*mockingly to* CYRANO].   It seems the nuptial night must
   be postponed.
CYRANO [*aside*].   He thinks this news will cut me to the quick.
CHRISTIAN [*to* ROXANE].   Your lips again! Once more!
CYRANO.   Come, come. Enough.

CHRISTIAN [*still kissing* ROXANE].   How hard it is to leave! You'll never
 know.
CYRANO [*trying to pull him away*].   I know.

 [*The sound of drums is heard in the distance.*]

DE GUICHE [*retiring to the background*].   The regiment is leaving.
ROXANE.   Oh! [*Holding on to* CHRISTIAN, *she turns to* CYRANO.]
 I trust him to you. Promise me his life
 Will never be in danger.
CYRANO.   I shall try.
 But I can scarcely promise—
ROXANE [*still holding* CHRISTIAN].   Promise me
 He will be careful.
CYRANO.   I shall do my best,
 But—
ROXANE.   He must not be cold during the siege.
CYRANO.   I'll do my very utmost, but—
ROXANE.   You will
 See that he's faithful.
CYRANO.   Oh, of course. But still—
ROXANE.   And see that he writes often.
CYRANO.   *That* I promise!

    [*The curtain falls.*]

Act IV

The Cadets of Gascony

The scene is the post occupied by the company of CARBON DE CASTEL-
  JALOUX *during the siege of Arras. In the background an embankment crosses the entire stage. Beyond this, there is a view of a wide
  plain stretching to the horizon. The countryside is covered with en-
  trenchments. The walls of Arras—its roofs silhouetted against the
  sky—are seen in the far distance.*

*Tents, guns, drums, and various pieces of armor are scattered about. Day
  is just beginning; the east is a faint yellow. Sentinels are stationed
  at various points. Watch-fires are still glowing.*

Wrapped in their cloaks, the Cadets of Gascony are sleeping. CARBON
  DE CASTEL-JALOUX *and* LE BRET *are on watch. They are pale and
  thin.* CHRISTIAN *is asleep among the others. He is in the foreground, his face wan in the light of the campfire.*

LE BRET.   It's terrible.

CARBON DE CASTEL-JALOUX.   Yes. Nothing left.

LE BRET.   By God!

CARBON.   Ssh! Swear in whispers. You might wake them up.
  [*to the* CADETS]
  Sleep. Sleep. The man who sleeps dreams that he eats.

LE BRET.   That is a shabby comfort for the sleepless.
  Such famine!

  [*Distant shots are heard.*]

  Devil take that firing!
  The sound will wake my boys. [*to* THE CADETS, *who lift their heads*]
  Sleep, boys, sleep on.
  [*They lie down again. The shooting increases, nearer this time.*]

A CADET [*moving*].   Again! The devil!

CARBON.   It is Cyrano,
    Returning, just as usual, through the lines.

[*The heads which had been raised sink back again.*]

A SENTINEL'S VOICE [*in the distance*].   Halt! Who goes there?
CYRANO'S VOICE.   Bergerac.
THE SENTINEL [*on the embankment*].   Who goes there?
CYRANO [*coming over the top*].   Bergerac, fool!
    [*As he comes forward,* LE BRET *goes anxiously to meet him.*]
LE BRET.   Well, thank the Lord!
CYRANO [*motioning him not to wake anyone*].   Keep still!
LE BRET.   You're wounded?
CYRANO.   No. You know quite well by now
    They miss me every morning—it's a habit.
LE BRET.   This passes everything! To risk your life
    Each day at dawn to get a letter through!
CYRANO.   I made a promise he would write—and often.
    [*He stops in front of* CHRISTIAN *and looks down at him.*]
    Asleep. And pale. If Roxane only knew
    He was half-dead of hunger—but still handsome.
LE BRET.   Go quickly, man, and get some sleep yourself.
CYRANO.   Don't scold, Le Bret. There's scarcely any risk.
    I know the Spanish lines; I've found a place
    Where they lie drunk each night.
LE BRET.   You should, some day,
    Try to bring food. God knows we need it here.
CYRANO.   To get through I must travel light. And yet
    Something is in the wind. If I am right
    The French will either dine or die tonight.
LE BRET.   Tell me.
CYRANO.   I am not sure—but you will see.
CARBON.   What kind of war is this! To die of hunger
    While doing the besieging. It's absurd!
LE BRET.   This is indeed a complicated war.
    We are besieging Arras—and, meanwhile,
    We're caught, trapped, and, to cap it all, besieged
    By our chief foe, the Cardinal-Prince of Spain.
CYRANO.   To bring this war full circle, some one should
    Come and besiege the Spanish Cardinal-Prince.
LE BRET.   I'm sorry but I cannot laugh.
CYRANO.   Ho! Ho!
LE BRET.   That one should risk a life like yours each day
    To smuggle through— [CYRANO *goes to his tent.*]

Where are you going now?

CYRANO.   Going, of course, to write another letter.

[*He lifts the tent-flap and disappears. For a moment there is complete silence. Day has dawned. There is a rosy light on the battlefield; the roofs and towers of Arras are gilded with the first rays. Cannon-fire breaks out, followed by the beating of drums in the distance. The noise is echoed by other and nearer drums. Reveille is sounded. The camp awakes to the murmuring of soldiers and the distant commands of officers.* THE CADETS *stir and stretch themselves.*]

A CADET [*sitting up*].   I'm hungry.

SECOND CADET.   I
Am dying.

[*All of them groan*]

CARBON.   Get up.

THIRD CADET.   Not another step!

FOURTH CADET.   Not even a gesture!

FIRST CADET [*looking at his reflection in a piece of armor*].   My tongue
is yellow;
The air is really indigestible!

SECOND CADET.   My barony for just a bit of cheese!

THIRD CADET.   If my poor stomach does not get some thing
To keep the gastric juice at work, I'll quit
And sulk, like old Achilles, in my tent.

FOURTH CADET.   Something—a crust of moldy bread!

CARBON [*going to* CYRANO's *tent and calling in a low voice*].   Cyrano!

THE CADETS.   We're dying—all of us.

CARBON [*whispering*].   Give me some help . . .
You who are always quick with gay replies,
Come, cheer them up.

SECOND CADET [*running over to* THE FIRST CADET *who is chewing something*].   What are you nibbling on?

FIRST CADET.   On cannon-wadding. They were frying some
In axle-grease. This place is short of game.

ANOTHER CADET [*entering*].   I've just been hunting.

ANOTHER CADET [*entering*].   I've been catching fish.

THE OTHERS [*rushing at the two who have just come in*].   What did
you bring? A carp? A nice fat pheasant?
Quick! Let us see!

THE FISHERMAN.   A minnow.

THE HUNTER.   One small sparrow.

THE OTHERS [*infuriated*].   Enough! Let us revolt!
CARBON.   Help, Cyrano!

[*It is now broad daylight.* CYRANO *comes out of his tent; a pen is
behind his ear, a book in his hand.*]

CYRANO.   What is the matter?
[*No one speaks.* CYRANO *addresses the* FIRST CADET.]
Why do you walk
With such slow steps?
FIRST CADET.   There's something in my heels
Which weighs them down.
CYRANO.   What can it be?
FIRST CADET.   My stomach.
CYRANO.   I have the same complaint.
FIRST CADET.   Does it not drag
And make you weak?
CYRANO.   It makes me thin—but tall.
SECOND CADET.   My teeth grow big.
CYRANO.   That will improve your bite.
THIRD CADET.   My belly's hollow.
CYRANO.   Use it for a drum.
FOURTH CADET.   I have a ringing in my ears.
CYRANO.   No, no.
An empty stomach, fellow, has no ears.
ANOTHER CADET.   Oh! For a bite of anything—with oil.
CYRANO [*taking off the* CADET'S *helmet and placing it in his hands*].
Your salad, friend.
ANOTHER CADET.   What is there to devour?
CYRANO [*throwing him the book he has been holding*].   The "Iliad."
FIRST CADET.   Our minister in Paris sits him down
To four fat meals a day.
CYRANO.   You think he should
Send you a brace of partridges?
FIRST CADET.   Why not?
And some wine, too! He has a cellarful.
CYRANO.   Richelieu, pass the Burgundy, if you please.
SECOND CADET.   I have a giant's appetite.
CYRANO.   Then feast
On your own fat.
FIRST CADET [*with a shrugging grimace*].   You're very quick with words.
But words are—words, and jests may lose their point.
CYRANO.   Don't scorn the point, my friend. When I must die
I hope to meet death 'neath some rosy sky,

With a good-ringing word for some good cause.
No bed of sickness, no slow failing flesh,
But a quick end—a worthy foeman's steel—
A pointed laughing word upon my lips
And the sword's pointed answer in my heart.
ALL THE CADETS.   But we are hungry!
CYRANO.   So, because you are,
　　You think of food, and nothing else but food!
　　Come, Bertrandou, play for these greedy gluttons.
　　You who were once a shepherd, hush the fife,
　　And play a country tune upon your flute.
　　Play something sweet and simple, where each note
　　Speaks of a little sister and of home;
　　An air unfolding slowly, like the smoke
　　From all the sleepy little villages;
　　A music which is still our native tongue.
　　[OLD BERTRANDOU *sits down and gets his flute ready.*]
　　That peaceful flute was once the warrior's fife.
　　Before it was a pipe, it was a grass—
　　A reed that played a minuet for birds . . .
　　Recall that happy time. Evoke once more
　　The pastures and the past.
　　[*The old man begins to play a folk-song of ancient* LANGUEDOC.]
　　Gascons, hear that!
　　Under his fingers it has ceased to be
　　The shrill fife of the camp; it has become
　　A woodwind of the woods. It is no call
　　To combat, but the soft and plaintive cry
　　Of wandering goatherds. Listen well! It is
　　The forest that you hear, the moors, the fields,
　　The plains, the shepherd in his red beret,
　　The tender evening at the river's edge,
　　The small forgotten voices of your youth.
　　It is—oh, Gascons—all of Gascony!

[THE CADETS *let their heads sink. Their eyes are full of dreams.
With the back of a sleeve or the corner of a cloak they furtively wipe
away their tears.*]

CARBON [*in a low voice to* CYRANO].   But you have made them weep!
CYRANO.   With homesickness—
　　A cleaner pain than hunger. When the flesh
　　Complains too much the spirit takes command.
　　It's good to see their change in suffering—

Better a heartache than a belly-ache . . .

CARBON.   But when you wring their hearts you soften them.

CYRANO.   Nonsense! The hero sleeping in their veins
Is quickly roused. [*He motions to the drummer to approach.*]
It only needs a touch. [*He makes a gesture and the drum rolls.*]

THE CADETS [*springing up*].   What? What is it?

CYRANO [*smiling*].   You see. They hear a drum—
And good-by dreams, farewell to memories,
To youth and old regrets, and home, and love.
All that the haunting flute had brought to mind
The harsh, imperative drum has driven away.

A CADET [*gazing into the distance*].   Aha! Here comes Monsieur de
Guiche.

THE OTHER CADETS [*muttering*].   Hoo! Hoo!

CYRANO [*grinning*].   A flattering sound!

FIRST CADET.   We're sick of him!

SECOND CADET.   He wears
A wide lace ruff above his heavy armor,
Playing the patrician, even on
The battlefield.

THIRD CADET.   As though it were the thing
To wear one's linen over steel!

FIRST CADET.   It would
Be handy for a boil upon the neck.

SECOND CADET.   Always the scheming courteous courtier!

THIRD CADET.   His uncle's nephew!

CARBON.   Still, he *is* a Gascon.

FIRST CADET.   A false one! I would never trust the man!
All honest Gascons are a little mad.
A reasonable Gascon is a fraud.
What's more, a man like that is dangerous!

LE BRET.   Yet he looks pale.

THIRD CADET.   And hungry, just like us.
But, since his armor's gay with silver gilt,
His cramping stomach glitters in the sun.

CYRANO [*quickly*].   Don't let him see that we are suffering.
Bring out the decks of cards, the dice, your pipes—

[*All* THE CADETS *begin to play cards and roll dice. Some use the
drum-heads for tables; others lay out the cards on their cloaks or
play on the ground. They light pipes and smoke nonchalantly.*]

I shall regale myself; I'll read Descartes.

[*He walks to and fro, reading a book he has taken from his pocket.*
DE GUICHE *enters. Everyone is occupied; everyone looks contented.*
DE GUICHE *is extremely pale. He goes over to* CARBON.]

DE GUICHE [*to* CARBON].   Good morning.
    [*He scrutinizes* CARBON *with satisfaction and says to himself:*]
    He is green!
CARBON [*looking at* DE GUICHE *with equal gratification*].   He is all
    eyes!
DE GUICHE [*scrutinizing* THE CADETS].
    So these are the loud malcontents . . . Yes, sirs,
    From every side I hear that I am mocked;
    That mere Cadets, uncultured country squires
    And petty barons, dare to jeer at me,
    Their colonel! That my courtesy is called
    Merely intrigue; that the lace collar worn
    Above my armor bothers them; in short,
    They are enraged and full of spleen to see
    That a born Gascon need not be a beggar!

    [*Silence.* THE CADETS *keep on playing.*]

    Now, shall I have you punished by your captain?
    No.
CARBON.   And, since I am free to maintain order,
    I do not punish.
DE GUICHE.   No?
CARBON.   They are my men.
    I will take orders—only orders of war.
DE GUICHE.   That is enough. [*He turns to* THE CADETS.]
    I am above your taunts.
    My bravery in battle is well known.
    At Bapaume yesterday you saw how I
    Compelled the Count of Bucquoi to fall back.
    Pouring my men on his, I charged three times
    And fell upon him like an avalanche.
CYRANO [*without looking up*].   And your white scarf?
DE GUICHE [*with surprise and gratification*].   You know the incident?
    It happened this way: As I turned my horse
    For the last charge, a pack of fugitives
    Dangerously dragged me near the enemy's lines.
    I might then have been taken prisoner
    And shot. But I thought quickly; dropped the scarf
    Which showed my military rank. And so

I fooled the Spaniards, rallied all my men,
Returned, and beat them! What do you say to that?

[*Although* THE CADETS *do not seem to be paying attention, their cards and dice-boxes remain suspended in the air. The smoke from their pipes is held in their cheeks.*]

CYRANO.   I'd say no odds or numbers ever made
Henry the Fourth conceal a single feather
From his panache, his proud white battle plume.

[CYRANO's *answer is silently but joyfully applauded. Cards are laid down; dice fall; and smoke is exhaled.*]

DE GUICHE.   Nevertheless the ruse succeeded.

[*Again everything is suspended—cards, dice, and breath.*]

CYRANO.   Yes;
But one does not so readily renounce
The pride—and danger—of being a mark
To shoot at.

[*Again the cards are played, the dice-boxes rattle and the smoke is blown with tremendous satisfaction.*]

Had I been there when the scarf
Fell to the ground—and here my courage, sir,
Differs from yours—I would have picked it up
And put it on.
DE GUICHE.   Of course! Another Gascon boast!
CYRANO.   A boast? Lend me the scarf. Tonight I will
Lead the attack and wear it like a plume.
DE GUICHE.   Boasting again! You know where the scarf is!
The enemy has it, at the river's brink,
Riddled with bullets, where no one would dare
To risk his life to fetch it.
CYRANO [*taking the scarf from his pocket and handling it to* DE GUICHE].   Here it is.

[*The silence is strange.* THE CADETS *attempt to repress their laughter behind cards and the shaking of dice-boxes.* DE GUICHE *turns and stares at them, and their faces freeze into an unnatural gravity. They resume their games. One of* THE CADETS *casually whistles the pleasant melody just played by the fifer.*]

DE GUICHE [*taking the scarf*].
Thank you. With this flimsy piece of cloth

I'll give the signal I had planned to make.
[*He climbs the embankment and waves the scarf a few times.*]
ALL THE CADETS.   What's that?
THE SENTINEL [*on the embankment*].
    A man down there has left the camp
    And run away.
DE GUICHE [*descending*].   It's a false Spanish spy
    In my employ, a very useful tool.
    The information which he gives our foe
    Is that which I give him.
CYRANO.   A nasty trick.
DE GUICHE [*blandly tying his scarf*].
    It serves its purpose. I was going to say—
    Oh, yes. Last night, to get some food for us,
    The Marshal went to Doullens, where the king's
    Provisions are. But to get safely back
    He took a section of our troops with him.
    Since half the camp is absent, it would be
    A pretty field-day for the enemy.
CARBON.   It is a good thing that our Spanish friends
    Know nothing of the absence.
DE GUICHE.   Oh, they know.
    They know—and will attack us.
CARBON.   How is that?
DE GUICHE.   My private spy warned me of an assault.
    He said, "I can direct the course of their attack.
    Where would you like the battle to be fought?
    You say—and I will tell them that the place
    Is thinly held. That's where the thrust will come."
    I answered, "Good. Get ready to leave camp.
    Watch for my signal—that will be the place."
CARBON.   Make ready, men.

[*All* THE CADETS *rise. They begin to buckle on belts and swords.*]

DE GUICHE.   It should come in an hour.
FIRST CADET.   Ah, well, we needn't hurry.

[*They all sit down again and proceed with their games.*]

DE GUICHE [*to* CARBON].   We need time.
    The Marshal will be back.
CARBON.   And to gain time?
DE GUICHE.   Your men will all be good enough
    To give their lives.

CYRANO.   And that is your revenge.

DE GUICHE.   I won't pretend that if I loved you all
    I might have chosen differently. But none
    Can boast like you—and so I serve my king
    By serving, at the same time, an old grudge.

CYRANO.   Allow us to express our gratitude.

DE GUICHE [*to* CYRANO].   Since you are fond of fighting all alone
    Against a hundred, you cannot complain
    About the odds.

CYRANO [*to* THE CADETS].   Comrades and gentlemen,
    Now we can give our Gascon coat of arms
    A brighter color. To the azure chevrons,
    Which now it bears, we'll add one more of gules:
    A rich blood-color which, till now, it lacked.

[DE GUICHE *draws* CARBON *to the back and speaks to him in a low
voice. Orders are given and preparations for the defense are made.*
CYRANO *goes to* CHRISTIAN, *who has been standing motionless with
his arms crossed.*]

CYRANO [*continuing, his hand on* CHRISTIAN's *shoulder*].   Christian?

CHRISTIAN [*shaking his head*].   Roxane!

CYRANO.   Too bad.

CHRISTIAN.   At least I wish
    I could have put a heartfelt, long good-bye
    In one last letter.

CYRANO.   Something made me feel
    That it would be today. [*He takes a piece of paper from his doublet.*]
    So I have written
    Your farewell note.

CHRISTIAN.   Let's see it.

CYRANO.   Do you wish—?

CHRISTIAN [*taking the letter*].   Why, certainly.
    [*He opens it, begins to read, and suddenly stops.*]
    Wait!

CYRANO.   What?

CHRISTIAN.   This little spot.

CYRANO [*taking the letter and examining it with a naïve expression*].
    A spot?

CHRISTIAN.   It is a tear!

CYRANO.   A tear? Oh, yes.
    Poets are their own victims. They are caught
    In their own web of words. This note I penned—
    It was so moving that it made me weep.

CHRISTIAN.   It made you weep?

CYRANO.   Yes. Death is not so bad.
　　But not to see her—never once again—
　　That is too horrible! For then I should—
　　I mean *we* should—*you* should—

CHRISTIAN [*snatching the letter*].   Give me that letter!

[*There is a far-off noise.*]

A SENTINEL'S VOICE.   Halt! Who goes there?

[*The noise becomes a confusion of firing, bells, and many voices.*]

CARBON.   What is it?

THE SENTINEL [*on the embankment*].   It's a coach!

[*Everyone rushes to see.*]

VOICES.   What! . . . In the camp! . . . It's coming in! . . . Look out!
　　It's from the enemy! . . . Fire on it! . . . No! . . .
　　The coachman shouts! . . . What did the coachman say? . . .
　　"On the King's service!"

[*Everyone is on the embankment, staring, as the carriage bells
sound nearer.*]

DE GUICHE.   What? The King?

CARBON.   Hats off!

DE GUICHE.   The King! Come on, you rowdies! Clear the way!
　　A king must enter in the proper style!

[*The coach rolls in at full speed. It is covered with mud and dust.
The curtains are drawn; two footmen are behind. The carriage stops
short.*]

CARBON [*shouting*].   Beat the salute!

[*The drums roll and all* THE CADETS *uncover.*]

Lower the step!

[*Two men hurry to the coach, but, just as they arrive, the door opens
and* ROXANE *steps out.*]

ROXANE [*brightly*].   Good morning!

[*All heads, which had been bowed low, are suddenly raised at the
sound of a woman's voice. The consternation is indescribable.*]

DE GUICHE.   On the King's service! You!

ROXANE.   The only king,

The king of love.
CYRANO.   Great God!
CHRISTIAN.   What made you come?
ROXANE.   It lasts too long, this siege.
CHRISTIAN.   But you! . . . And why?
ROXANE.   I'll tell you everything in time.

[*At the first sound of her voice* CYRANO *has remained motionless, rooted to the ground. He seems afraid to raise his eyes.*]

CYRANO.   Dear God!
How can I look at her?
DE GUICHE.   You can't stay here.
ROXANE [*gaily*].   Oh yes, I can! Will someone bring a drum?

[THE CADETS *bring forward a drum and she seats herself on it.*]

There! Thank you.
[*She laughs.*] Look! They fired upon my coach!
It looks just like a pumpkin, doesn't it?
As in the fairy-tale, complete with rats
Turned into handsome footmen.
[*She throws a kiss to* CHRISTIAN.] Ah! Good morning!
I must say none of you look very gay . . .
How far to Arras? [*She notices* CYRANO.]
Cousin, I am charmed.
CYRANO.   Thank you. But how—?
ROXANE.   How did I find the army?
Simple enough. I merely followed where
I saw the most destruction. I would not
Have thought such scenes of horror possible.
Believe me, sirs, if this is how you serve
The King of France, I serve a better monarch.
CYRANO.   But this is madness. Where did you get through?
ROXANE.   Where? Through the Spanish lines.
FIRST CADET.   An ugly lot.
DE GUICHE.   How did you pass the lines?
LE BRET.   Wasn't it hard?
ROXANE.   Not hard at all. The coach drove on full speed.
And when some fierce hidalgo showed his face
I showed my sweetest smile. Since Spaniards are—
No disrespect to Frenchmen—the most gallant,
I passed with ease.
CARBON.   Surely, that smile of yours
Is a good passport. But they must have asked

Where you were going, and the reason why.
ROXANE.   They asked it frequently. I always said,
   "I'm going to meet my lover." At that word
   The roughest-looking Spaniard of them all
   Would close the door and, with a gesture that a king
   Might envy, brush aside the bristling guns
   Levelled at me. Then, full of stately grace,
   Clanking his spurs, waving his broad-brimmed hat
   So that the long plumes swept the air, he'd bow
   And "Señorita," he would say, "pass on."
CHRISTIAN.   But still, Roxane—
ROXANE.   Forgive me that I said "my lover."
   You see, if I had said "my husband"—ah!
   No one would let me pass.
CHRISTIAN.   But—
ROXANE.   What is wrong?
DE GUICHE.   You must go.
ROXANE.   I?
CYRANO.   And quickly.
LE BRET.   Right away.
CHRISTIAN.   Indeed, you must.
ROXANE.   But why?
CHRISTIAN [*hesitating*].   Because—
CYRANO [*also embarrassed*].   It seems
   In just about three quarters of an hour—
DE GUICHE [*nervously*].   Or less—
CARBON [*urgently*].   It would be better—
LE BRET [*anxiously*].   Or you might—
ROXANE [*placidly*].   I see. You're going to fight. I shall remain.
ALL.   No! No!
ROXANE [*throwing herself into* CHRISTIAN'*s arms*].
   He is my husband. I will die
   With him.
CHRISTIAN.   Your blazing eyes are beautiful.
ROXANE.   I'll tell you why.
DE GUICHE.   This post's a mortal risk.
ROXANE.   A mortal risk!
CYRANO.   What's more, he made it so.
ROXANE [*to* DE GUICHE].   So! You would make a widow of me here!
DE GUICHE.   Madame, I swear—
ROXANE.   Now I am furious!
   I'll never leave. Besides, it's entertaining.
CYRANO.   Has our *précieuse* become a heroine?

ROXANE.   Monsieur de Bergerac, I am your cousin.

A CADET.   We will defend you well.

ROXANE [*excitedly*].   I know you will!

ANOTHER CADET.   The whole camp smells of fragrant orris root!

ROXANE.   And, luckily, I have worn a hat
Which should look charming on a battlefield.
[*Looking pointedly at* DE GUICHE]
But might it not be wiser if the Count
Were to retire. They may attack at once.

DE GUICHE.   Impertinence! . . . I must inspect the guns
And shall return. You'd better change your mind.

ROXANE.   Never!

CHRISTIAN [*pleadingly*].   Roxane!

ROXANE.   No!

FIRST CADET [*to the others*].   She is going to stay!

[THE CADETS *run, jostling each other, trying to make themselves
presentable.*]

THE CADETS.   A comb! . . . A brush! . . . Some soap! . . . A pin! . . .
Some thread! . . .
My clothing's torn! . . . Lend me your mirror! . . . Quick! . . .
My gloves! . . . Your curling iron! . . . Razor! . . . Here! . . .

ROXANE [*to* CYRANO, *who is still arguing with her*].   Nothing will make
me stir. This is my place.

[*Meanwhile* CARBON *has, like the rest, tidied himself up. He has
tightened his buckle, dusted his clothes, brushed his hat, fluffed out
his plumes, and drawn on his gauntlets. He approaches* ROXANE
with much ceremony.]

CARBON.   Since you are so determined, and will stay,
Perhaps I should present the gentlemen
Who are about to have the honor of dying
Before your eyes. [ROXANE *bows and, leaning on* CHRISTIAN's *arm,
stands waiting while* CARBON *presents his men.*]
Baron de Peyrescous
De Colignac.

THE CADET [*bowing*].   Madame . . .

CARBON [*continuing*].   Baron de Casterac
De Cahuzac . . . Vidame de Malgouyre
Estressac Lésbas d'Escarbiot . . .
Chevalier d'Antignac-Juzet . . . Baron Hillot
De Blagnac-Saléchan de Castel Crabioules . . .

ROXANE.   How many names apiece have each of you?

BARON HILLOT.   Oh, more than we can count.
CARBON [*to* ROXANE].   Do me a favor
　　Open the hand which holds your handkerchief.
ROXANE [*opens her hand and the handkerchief falls*].   But why—?
　　[*The* CADETS *rush toward the handkerchief, but* CARBON *picks it up.*]
CARBON.   My company always lacked a flag;
　　Now it will fly the proudest flag of all.
ROXANE [*smiling*].   It's rather small.
CARBON [*tying the handkerchief to the staff of his captain's lance*].   But
　　it is royal lace!
FIRST CADET [*to the others*].   Seeing so sweet a face I could die happy
　　If I had something in my stomach first.
CARBON [*overhearing him, indignantly*].
　　For shame! To speak of food when a refined
　　And exquisite young lady—
ROXANE.   He is right.
　　This air is sharp; my appetite is keen.
　　I'd like some pâtés, cold meats, a good wine—
　　Will someone bring it here?
FIRST CADET.   What! All of that!
SECOND CADET.   Good Lord, where shall we find it?
ROXANE [*calmly*].   In my carriage.
ALL.   What!
ROXANE.   Look a little closer at my coachman.
　　You'll recognize a most unusual man;
　　One who can serve your sauces hot or cold.
THE CADETS [*rushing to the carriage with joyful cries*].   It's Ragueneau!
ROXANE.   Poor, famished men of war!
CYRANO [*kissing her hand*].   Good fairy! [RAGUENEAU *on the driver's seat addresses* THE CADETS *like a showman.*]
RAGUENEAU.   Gentlemen!
THE CADETS.   Bravo! Bravo!
RAGUENEAU.   The Spaniards were a little more than fair:
　　Letting the fairy—and the good fare—through.

　　[THE CADETS *applaud, while* CYRANO *goes over to* CHRISTIAN.]

CYRANO.   Christian!
RAGUENEAU.   So, overcome with gallantry,
　　They did not stoop to see—[*He draws a dish from under the seat
　　and holds it up triumphantly.*]
　　the galantine!

[*Renewed applause as the galantine of fowl is passed from hand to hand.*]

CYRANO [*to* CHRISTIAN *in a whisper*].   A word with you. It's most important.

RAGUENEAU.   And Venus occupied their eyes so well,
Diana fooled them with her little—
[*He holds up a leg of mutton*] game!

[*The leg of mutton is passed around by twenty enthusiastic hands.*]

CYRANO [*low but persistently, to* CHRISTIAN].   You've got to listen.

ROXANE [*to* THE CADETS *who are bringing armfuls of food from the carriage*].   Lay it on the ground. [*She spreads a cloth on the grass, assisted by the two imperturbable footmen who were behind the coach. Then she turns to* CHRISTIAN *just as* CYRANO *was drawing him away.*]
Make yourself useful here!

[CHRISTIAN *comes to help her, while* CYRANO *seems worried.*]

RAGUENEAU.   Peacock—with truffles!

FIRST CADET [*grinning from ear to ear as he cuts a huge slice of ham*].
By God! Before we die at least we'll have
One final gorge!
[*Catching* ROXANE's *eye he quickly corrects himself.*]
I mean—a royal feast.

RAGUENEAU [*tossing cushions from the carriage*].   You'll find those cushions full of roasted birds.

[*There is a renewed tumult of joyful exclamations as* THE CADETS *rip open the cushions.*]

THIRD CADET.   Ah! Thank you, landlord!

RAGUENEAU [*handing out bottles of wine*].   Flasks of ruby red
And topaz yellow.

ROXANE [*throwing a folded tablecloth at* CYRANO's *head*].
Catch! Unfold that cloth!
Be quick! We cannot wait!

RAGUENEAU [*waving one of the lamps he has pulled from the coach*].
Each carriage lamp
Is quite a little larder.

CYRANO [*to* CHRISTIAN, *as they arrange the cloth between them*].
I must speak
To you before you speak a word to her.

RAGUENEAU [*rhetorically*].   Even the handle of my whip conceals
A monster sausage—specialty of Arles.

ROXANE [*serving the wine*].   Since we must die, let us die merrily,
     Laughing at all the others less well fed.
     Gascons deserve the best of everything.
     But if de Guiche comes—not a word of this.
     [*She goes from one to another.*]
     There! There! Don't eat so fast. There's time enough.
     Come, take a little wine . . . Why do you weep?
FIRST CADET.   It's all too wonderful!
ROXANE.   Hush! Red or white? . . .
     Bread for Monsieur de Carbon . . . Here's your knife . . .
     Another plate? . . . A little crust? . . . A wing? . . .
     Taste the champagne . . . Try just a little more?
CYRANO [*following and helping her, his arms full of plates*].   She is
     adorable.
ROXANE [*going to* CHRISTIAN].   What would you like?
CHRISTIAN.   Nothing.
ROXANE.   Please—try this sweetcake, dipped in wine.
CHRISTIAN [*trying to detain her*].   First tell me why you came.
ROXANE.   After I've served
     These poor unlucky fellows. By and by—
LE BRET [*has gone to the rear of the stage to pass some bread on the end
     of his lance to* THE SENTINEL *on the embankment. Suddenly he
     cries:*]   De Guiche!
CYRANO.   Quick! Hide the bottles, dishes, pots,
     Platters and pans! Conceal all trace of food
     And look unconscious.

     [*In a flash everything vanishes, pushed into tents, hidden under
     cloaks, stuffed into doublets or even crammed into hats.* DE GUICHE
     *enters hastily, stops suddenly—and sniffs. There is a most suspi-
     cious silence.*]

DE GUICHE.   Ah! It smells good here.
FIRST CADET [*humming*].   La, la, la, la . . .
DE GUICHE [*scrutinizing him*].   Is anything the matter?
     You look quite red.
FIRST CADET.   Do I? It's nothing much.
     My battle-blood is up . . . Let's fight . . .
SECOND CADET.   Poum, poum . . .
DE GUICHE [*turning*].   And what is that?
SECOND CADET [*somewhat intoxicated*].   Nothing. A little song.
DE GUICHE.   You're strangely gay, my lad.
SECOND CADET.   It is the smell
     Of danger which delights me.

DE GUICHE [*to* CARBON, *intending to give him an order*].   Captain, I—
  By God! But you look cheerful, too!
CARBON [*turning crimson and hiding a bottle awkwardly behind his
  back*].   I?—Oh!
DE GUICHE.   There is one cannon left. I've placed it there.
  [*He points to a place offstage.*]
  Your men can use it if they're badly pressed.
SECOND CADET [*reeling a little*].   A sweet attention.
THIRD CADET [*smiling graciously*].   Such solicitude!
DE GUICHE.   Are you all mad! [*drily*]
  Since you're unused to cannon,
  Look out for the recoil.
FIRST CADET.   Oh, pfft!
DE GUICHE [*outraged*].   Look here—!
FIRST CADET.   A Gascon cannon never will recoil!
DE GUICHE [*seizing him by the arm and shaking him*].   You're drunk!
  . . . With what?
FIRST CADET [*grandly*].   Gunpowder's heavy fumes.
DE GUICHE [*shrugs his shoulders, pushes* THE CADET *aside, and turns
  to* ROXANE].   Madam, have you made up your mind to go?
ROXANE.   I shall remain.
DE GUICHE.   I warn you—leave.
ROXANE.   I'll stay.
DE GUICHE.   If that's the way it is, give me a gun.
CARBON.   What for?
DE GUICHE.   I'll stay here, too.
CYRANO.   Well, this is more
  Than mere bravado. It is bravery.
FIRST CADET.   In spite of all your lace, you *are* a Gascon.
DE GUICHE.   I've never left a woman who's in danger.
SECOND CADET [*to* THE FIRST CADET].   You know, I think the man
  deserves a bite.

  [*As if by magic, all the food reappears.*]

DE GUICHE [*with widening eyes*].   It's food!
THIRD CADET.   It comes from under every cloak.
DE GUICHE [*mastering his hunger, with great haughtiness*].   You'd
  think I'd eat your leavings!
CYRANO [*saluting him*].   Very good.
  You're making rapid progress.
DE GUICHE.   I shall fast
  And fight the better for it.
FIRST CADET.   Ah, there speaks

The Gascon—with a Gascon accent, too.
DE GUICHE [*smiling and speaking broadly*].   What? I?
FIRST CADET.   Hurrah! He's one of us!

[*They dance with delight. After disappearing for a moment,* CARBON
*comes from behind the embankment. He points to a bristling row of
pikes, the points of which are seen above the rampart.*]

CARBON.   I've put
My pikemen there. The men are resolute.
DE GUICHE [*bowing to* ROXANE].   Will you accept my hand for the re-
view?

[ROXANE *takes his hand and they go up the embankment. The rest
uncover and follow them.* CHRISTIAN *hurries over to* CYRANO. *There
is a cry offstage as* ROXANE *appears on the rampart, the pikes dip in
a salute, and* ROXANE *bows.*]

CHRISTIAN [*to* CYRANO].   Talk quickly now. Why all the secrecy?
CYRANO.   In case Roxane—
CHRISTIAN.   Go on.
CYRANO.   Should speak about
The letters . . .
CHRISTIAN.   Yes. I know.
CYRANO.   Don't show surprise.
CHRISTIAN.   At what?
CYRANO.   At anything she says. You see—
I must explain—Lord! It is nothing much—
On seeing her today I thought of it—
You have—
CHRISTIAN.   Go on.
CYRANO.   You have been writing her
Oftener than you know.
CHRISTIAN.   What!
CYRANO.   Yes. I thought
I understood your passion; so,
As your interpreter, I wrote sometimes
Without informing you.
CHRISTIAN.   Ah!
CYRANO.   That is all.
It was quite simple.
CHRISTIAN.   But we are hemmed in.
How did you manage—?
CYRANO.   I got through by dawn.
CHRISTIAN [*folding his arms*].   And that was simple, too? . . . If I may ask.

How often did I write her? Twice a week? . . .
Three times? . . . Four times? . . .
CYRANO.   Oh, oftener.
CHRISTIAN.   Each day?
CYRANO.   Yes, every day. And twice a day.
CHRISTIAN [*violently*].   And this
Inflamed you so that, drunk with joy,
You went and risked your life—
CYRANO.   Hush! Here she comes.

[*As* ROXANE *enters,* CYRANO *hurries into his tent. In the back-ground, the* CADETS *go back and forth while* CARBON *and* DE GUICHE *give them orders.*]

ROXANE [*running eagerly to* CHRISTIAN].   Christian! At last!
CHRISTIAN [*seizing her hands*].   At last you'll tell me why
You came to join me here by fearful roads,
Through dangerous ranks and ribald soldiery.
ROXANE.   My love, your letters brought me here.
CHRISTIAN.   What's that?
ROXANE.   And if I risked my life, the fault is yours.
Your letters made me dizzier than wine.
All of them! All this month! And every one
More thrilling than the one preceding it!
CHRISTIAN.   What! For a few love letters—!
ROXANE.   Do not mock.
You do not know their power. Ever since
That magic night beneath my balcony
When, in a voice that I had never heard,
Your soul spoke out, you have been my beloved.
And now, your perfect letters all this month!
Your voice was in them, the same tender voice,
So warm, so near, and oh, so sheltering!
No wonder that I hurried to your side!
Had old Ulysses written as you wrote
Penelope would have flung aside her loom
And, wild in love as Helen, rushed to join him.
CHRISTIAN.   But—
ROXANE.   Over and over again, I read them all.
They made me faint. They made me long for you.
Each separate page was like a trembling leaf
Loosed from your soul. I felt each burning word
Had come alive, powerful and sincere.
CHRISTIAN.   Sincere and powerful? . . . And you could feel

  All that, Roxane?
ROXANE.   Ah, how I felt it all!
CHRISTIAN.   And so you came—?
ROXANE.   Because I could not stay away.
    Oh, Christian, my dear lord, you'd lift me up
    Were I to cast myself down at your feet.
    But you could never lift the soul that suffers here.
    I came to ask forgiveness—and my plea
    Is urgent now that death is threatening.
    Pardon me for the wrong I did our love
    In loving you because you were so fair.
CHRISTIAN [*alarmed*].   Roxane!
ROXANE.   That was at first. Then, later on—
    Less foolish, like a bird that spreads its wings
    Before it dares to fly—I loved your soul.
    Your beauty held me still. And so I loved
    Beauty and soul together.
CHRISTIAN.   Ah! And now?
ROXANE.   Now that I know your greater, nobler self,
    I love you only for your shining soul.
CHRISTIAN [*frightened*].   Roxane!
ROXANE.   And so be happy. To be loved
    For beauty is a poor reward; it is
    To love a mask, a temporary dress,
    A sham unworthy of the loving heart.
    Your beauty which, at first, bedazzled me,
    Now that I see more clearly, disappears
    And is not seen at all.
CHRISTIAN.   Oh!
ROXANE.   Do you doubt
    Your final triumph?
CHRISTIAN [*deeply hurt*].   Oh! Roxane!
ROXANE.   I know
    You find it hard to understand such love.
CHRISTIAN.   I do not want such love! I want the love
    Which simply—
ROXANE.   Loves you for your handsome face?
    No, no! My love is deeper, worthier.
CHRISTIAN.   But our first love was all that one could ask.
ROXANE.   Oh, you are wrong! Now that I love you more,
    I love you best. It is the inner you
    That I adore and worship. Oh, my own,
    Even were you less brilliant—

CHRISTIAN. Please, Roxane!
ROXANE. I'd love you still. If you should suddenly
    Lose all your beauty—
CHRISTIAN. Do not say it.
ROXANE. Yes.
    I say it, and I mean it.
CHRISTIAN. If I were—
    Ugly?
ROXANE. It would not seem like ugliness.
CHRISTIAN. Oh, God!
ROXANE. That means your joy is greater?
CHRISTIAN [*choking*]. Yes.
ROXANE. Then what disturbs you?
CHRISTIAN. Nothing . . . Just a word . . .
    A moment . . .
ROXANE. But—
CHRISTIAN [*indicating a group of* CADETS *in the background*].
    Our love takes you away
    From those poor fellows. They're about to die.
    Go, smile on them.
ROXANE [*deeply touched*]. My own considerate Christian!

[*She goes over to* THE CADETS, *who crowd worshipfully around her.*
CHRISTIAN *approaches* CYRANO's *tent and calls.*]

CHRISTIAN. Cyrano!
CYRANO [*reappears, armed for battle*]. What's the matter? You look
    pale.
CHRISTIAN. She does not love me.
CYRANO. Nonsense!
CHRISTIAN. It is you
    She really loves.
CYRANO. Absurd!
CHRISTIAN. She loves my soul
    And nothing but my soul.
CYRANO. Oh, no!
CHRISTIAN. Oh, yes!
    You are the one she loves—and you love her!
CYRANO. I?
CHRISTIAN. Yes. I know.
CYRANO. It's true.
CHRISTIAN. You love her madly.
CYRANO. Madly, and worse.
CHRISTIAN. Then tell her so.

CYRANO. Not I.

CHRISTIAN. Why not?

CYRANO. Look at my face.

CHRISTIAN. She'd still love me
  Even though I were ugly.

CYRANO. She said that?

CHRISTIAN. She did.

CYRANO. Well, I am glad she told you that.
  But do not be deceived. It is a sweet
  And pleasant thought—but it is just a thought.
  Never accept it as a truth, and never grow
  Ugly or plain. She'd blame me for that, too!

CHRISTIAN. That's what I want to know.

CYRANO. Ridiculous!

CHRISTIAN. Yes. Let her choose. Go; tell her everything.

CYRANO. No, no. Spare me the torture.

CHRISTIAN. Is it fair
  For me to wreck your happiness because
  I chance to be good-looking?

CYRANO. And should I
  Destroy your dream because a whim of nature's
  Gave me a way with words, a trick of saying
  All of the things you feel?

CHRISTIAN. First, tell her all.

CYRANO. My friend, why do you tempt me?

CHRISTIAN. I am tired
  Of being my own rival.

CYRANO. Christian! Stop!

CHRISTIAN. The marriage—secret—without witnesses—
  Can simply be annulled—if we survive.

CYRANO. My God! The man persists!

CHRISTIAN. Yes. I must be
  Loved for myself—just that—or not at all . . .
  I'm going to see what's happening out there,
  Where the line ends. You stay here. I'll return.
  And when I do—But, meanwhile, speak to her
  And let her choose between us.

CYRANO. It will be
  You—only you.

CHRISTIAN. Well, I can hope. [*He calls.*]
  Roxane!

CYRANO. No! No!

ROXANE [*entering anxiously*]. What is the matter?

CHRISTIAN. Cyrano
Has an important piece of news for you.

[CHRISTIAN *leaves abruptly as* ROXANE *hurries over to* CYRANO.]

ROXANE [*worried*]. Important news?
CYRANO [*at a loss*]. He's gone.
[*to* ROXANE] Oh, really nothing!
He sees—you know—importance in a breath.
ROXANE [*quickly*]. Perhaps he doubted what I said. I know
That's what it is. I felt he questioned it.
CYRANO [*taking her hand*]. And are you sure you told him the whole
truth?
ROXANE. You mean that I would love him even if—?

[*She hesitates a second;* CYRANO *smiles sadly.*]

CYRANO. It's hard to say the word right to my face?
ROXANE. But—
CYRANO. It won't hurt me. Say it. Even if—
ROXANE. Even if he were ugly! I said that.

[*The sound of firing is heard, but* CYRANO *will not be interrupted.*]

CYRANO [*urgently*]. Hideous?
ROXANE. Hideous.
CYRANO. Disfigured?
ROXANE. Yes.
CYRANO. Grotesque?
ROXANE. He would not seem grotesque to me.
CYRANO. You'd love him still the same?
ROXANE. And even more.
CYRANO [*to himself, in a frenzy of anticipation*].
My God! Can it be true? Can happiness
Be mine at last?
[*to* ROXANE] Listen, Roxane. For I—
LE BRET [*entering suddenly*]. Cyrano!
CYRANO. What!
LE BRET. Come here. [*He whispers something.*]
CYRANO. My God! [*He drops* ROXANE'*s hand and stands stupefied.*]
ROXANE. What's wrong?
CYRANO [*stunned, to himself*]. This is the end.

[*The musket-fire increases.*]

ROXANE. Why are they firing now?
[ROXANE *goes back to the rampart and tries to look over it.*]

CYRANO.   It's finished. I can never let her know.

ROXANE [*about to leap over the battlements*].   I must find out what's happening!

CYRANO [*rushing to stop her*].   Nothing!

[*A few* CADETS *enter hiding something which they are carrying. They surround the object and conceal it from* ROXANE. CYRANO *draws her away.*]

ROXANE.   Those men—?

CYRANO.   Never mind them.

ROXANE.   A while ago
You said that there was something I should know.

CYRANO.   I did? Some trifle. I've forgotten it.
A little less than nothing . . . I can swear
That Christian's nature, like his soul, was great—
Is great—

ROXANE.   Was—? [*She screams.*]
Oh! [*She rushes forward toward the group of cadets, pushing everyone aside.*]

CYRANO.   What an unhappy end!

ROXANE [*sees* CHRISTIAN *wrapped in his cloak*].   Christian!

LE BRET [*to* CYRANO].   Struck by the enemy's first shot.

[ROXANE *throws herself on* CHRISTIAN'S *body. The firing breaks out in greater force. Battle noises are heard: roll of drums, clash of arms, and general tumult.*]

CARBON [*sword in air*].   It's the attack! To arms!

[CARBON *goes over the rampart, followed by* THE CADETS.]

ROXANE.   Christian!

CARBON'S VOICE [*on the other side of the embankment*].   Prepare!

ROXANE.   Christian!

CARBON'S VOICE.   Fall in!

ROXANE.   Christian!

CARBON'S VOICE.   Your fuses—fix!

[RAGUENEAU *runs up with a helmet full of water.*]

CHRISTIAN [*in a dying voice*].   Roxane!

[*Distractedly* ROXANE *tears a piece of linen from her bodice, dips it into the water, bathes the wound and tries to stop the bleeding.* CYRANO *bends over* CHRISTIAN *and whispers in his ear.*]

CYRANO [*to* CHRISTIAN].   I've told her everything. It's you

And only you, she loves—no matter what.

[CHRISTIAN *closes his eyes.*]

ROXANE.   Oh, my dear love!

CARBON'S VOICE.   Draw ramrods!

ROXANE [*to* CYRANO].   Does he breathe?

CARBON'S VOICE.   Open the charges with your teeth!

ROXANE.   But now
I feel his cheek grow cold against my own.

CARBON'S VOICE.   Aim!

ROXANE.   There's a letter on him. [*She opens it.*]
Oh! For me!

CARBON'S VOICE.   Fire! [*The musket shots redouble, followed by cries, shouts and the noise of battle.*]

CYRANO [*trying to release his hand, which the kneeling* ROXANE *has been holding*].   But, Roxane, the battle has begun.

ROXANE [*holding him back*].   Stay with me just a moment. He is dead.
You knew him best—you were the only one. [*She weeps quietly.*]
Was he not something wonderful—unique?

CYRANO [*standing up bare-headed*].   Yes, Roxane.

ROXANE.   A great, inspired poet?

CYRANO.   Yes, Roxane.

ROXANE.   A large and noble mind?

CYRANO.   Yes, Roxane.

ROXANE.   A lofty heart that soared
Above the cheap and trivial run of things?
A soul both charming and magnificent?

CYRANO [*doggedly*].   Yes, Roxane.

ROXANE [*throwing herself with a cry on* CHRISTIAN's *corpse*].   Now he
is dead!

CYRANO [*drawing his sword*].   And here, today,
I would die, too. Why should I live, when she
Is mourning for me without knowing it?

[*Trumpets sound in the distance.* DE GUICHE *appears bare-headed on the embankment. He is wounded in the forehead.*]

DE GUICHE [*shouting*].   Hold out a little longer! Help is coming!
The French are entering the camp with food!
The trumpet was the signal!

ROXANE.   Blood and tears!
His blood upon the letter—and his tears!

A VOICE [*outside*].   Surrender!

THE CADETS.   Never!

[RAGUENEAU, *having climbed up on his carriage, is watching the progress of the battle near the embankment.*]

RAGUENEAU.   It is growing worse!

CYRANO [*to* DE GUICHE].   Take her away! I'm going to join the charge!

ROXANE [*kissing the letter, in a strangled voice*].   His blood! His tears!

RAGUENEAU [*jumping from the coach and hurrying to* ROXANE].   She's fainted!

DE GUICHE [*on the embankment, to* THE CADETS].   Hold your ground!

A VOICE [*outside*].   Throw down your arms!

THE CADETS [*shouting*].   No! Never!

CYRANO [*to* DE GUICHE].   You have proved
Your bravery. [*He points to Roxane.*]
Fly, and take her away.

[DE GUICHE *rushes to* ROXANE *and lifts her in his arms.*]

DE GUICHE.   I'll do it. If we only hold them off
A little longer we will have them trapped.

CYRANO.   That's good.

[DE GUICHE, *assisted by* RAGUENEAU, *carries off the unconscious* ROXANE]

Farewell, Roxane.

[*There is a tumult of shouts and screams. Some of* THE CADETS *reappear, wounded, and fall upon the stage.* CYRANO, *rushing into battle, is stopped by* CARBON DE CASTEL-JALOUX, *covered with blood.*]

CARBON.   We're giving way.
The line is breaking. I've been wounded twice.

CYRANO [*shouting*].   Hold on, boys! Gascons never turn their backs!
[*to* CARBON, *whom he is supporting*] Don't be afraid. I've two deaths to avenge:
My friend Christian's—and my dead happiness. [CYRANO *flourishes the lance to which* ROXANE's *handkerchief is tied.*]
Fly, little flag that bears her monogram!
[*He plants it in the ground and cries to* THE CADETS.]
Fall on them, Gascons. Mow them down! [*To the Fifer*]
Play! Play!

[*The fife plays. The wounded men are roused; some of them struggle to their feet. A few* CADETS *rally around* CYRANO *and the little flag. The coach is crowded with men and, bristling with arms, becomes a little fort. A* CADET *appears on the top of the embankment and,*] *fighting while he retreats, shouts to the others.*]

THE CADET.   They're storming the last rampart! Here they come!
[*He drops dead.*]

CYRANO.   We'll give them a salute!

[*A formidable array of enemy troops suddenly swarms over the embankment. The Imperialist flags are raised on the ramparts.*]

Fire on them!

A SHOUT [*in the enemy's ranks*].   Fire!

[THE CADETS *fire and there is a deadly answering volley.* CADETS *fall on every side.*]

A SPANISH OFFICER [*removing his helmet in salute*].   Who are these madmen, unafraid of death?

CYRANO [*stands erect and, in a rain of bullets, faces the officer and recites:*]   These are Cadets of Gascony,
     Of Carbon de Castel-Jaloux.
Fighting and lying shamelessly,
 [*He plunges toward the embankment, followed by a few survivors.*]
These are Cadets—

[*The rest is lost in the tumult of battle. The din increases as the curtain falls.*]

Act V

Cyrano's Gazette

THE TIME *is fifteen years later; it is 1655. The place is a park belonging to the Sisters of the Cross, in Paris.*

Magnificent foliage. To the left, the house; a vast staircase which opens on to various doors. In the center is one particularly huge tree which stands alone. On the right is a semi-circular stone seat flanked by boxwood shrubs.

The background is crossed by a shaded avenue of chestnut trees leading on the right to a chapel partly disclosed through the branches. Vistas of lawns, walks, thickets, little groves and a clear sky are glimpsed through a curtain of leaves.

A small side door of the chapel opens on a colonnade, covered with reddening vines. It is autumn. Most of the foliage is turning yellow and red above the bright grass. The yews and box trees are still green, but dead leaves lie under every tree. Dry leaves cover the steps and stone seat and are scattered over the ground where they crackle under foot.

Toward the right, between the stone seat and the tree, there is a large embroidery frame with a small chair in front of it. Beneath it are baskets filled with skeins and balls of wool. A piece of tapestry has been started.

As the curtain rises the nuns are coming and going in the little park. Some of them are sitting around an older nun on the stone seat. Leaves are falling.

SISTER MARTHA [*to* MOTHER MARGARET].
 This morning Sister Claire looked in her mirror
 Not only once but twice, to see how well
 Her head-dress suited her.
MOTHER MARGARET. That was not good.

SISTER CLAIRE.　But Sister Martha slyly took a plum
　　Out of the tart this morning. I could see.
MOTHER MARGARET.　That was not nice.
SISTER CLAIRE.　But such a little glance!
SISTER MARTHA.　And such a tiny plum!
MOTHER MARGARET.　Still, I shall tell
　　Your sins to Monsieur Cyrano today.
SISTER CLAIRE.　Oh, don't! He will make fun of us!
SISTER MARTHA.　He'll say
　　That nuns are very vain.
SISTER CLAIRE.　And very greedy.
MOTHER MARGARET [*smiling indulgently*].　And very sweet.
SISTER CLAIRE.　But is it really true,
　　Dear Mother Margaret, that he has come
　　Here to the convent every Saturday
　　For ten long years?
MOTHER MARGARET.　Longer than that, my child.
　　He's come here ever since his cousin came
　　To mix the worldly mourning of her crêpe
　　With our coarse linen, like a black-winged bird
　　Among a flock of white and twittering doves.
　　And that was fourteen years ago.
SISTER MARTHA.　Ever since she took refuge from the world
　　Here, in this cloister, with her prodigal grief,
　　He is the only one who can make her smile.
ALL THE SISTERS [*interrupting each other*].
　　He is so quaint! . . . It's lively when he comes! . . .
　　He teases all of us! . . . He is so kind! . . .
　　We'll make him pâtés with angelica.
SISTER MARTHA.　We like him very much—but he is not
　　A good, church-going Catholic.
SISTER CLAIRE.　Well, then,
　　We will convert him!
THE OTHER SISTERS.　Yes!
MOTHER MARGARET.　That I forbid.
　　Were you to try, and were you to succeed,
　　He might repent—and come here much less often.
SISTER MARTHA.　But . . . if he does not know God . . .
MOTHER MARGARET.　Never fear.
　　God knows him very well.
SISTER MARTHA.　Each Saturday
　　When he arrives he tells me boastfully,
　　"Yesterday—Friday—sister, I ate meat!"

MOTHER MARGARET.   He tells you that? Well, this last Saturday
  He had not eaten anything at all
  For two whole days!
SISTER MARTHA.   Mother!
MOTHER MARGARET.   He's very poor.
SISTER MARTHA.   Who told you this?
MOTHER MARGARET.   His friend, Monsieur Le Bret.
SISTER MARTHA.   And is there none to help?
MOTHER MARGARET.   He is too proud;
  Any assistance would be an offense.

[ROXANE *appears in one of the shaded walks at the back of the*
stage. She is clothed completely in black: widow's cap and long veil.
DE GUICHE, *aging but still impressive-looking, accompanies her.*
They walk slowly. MOTHER MARGARET *rises.*]

We must go in now. Madame Madeleine
Strolls in the garden with her visitor.
SISTER MARTHA [*whispering to* SISTER CLAIRE].   Is it the Duke and
  Marshal of Grammont?
SISTER CLAIRE.   Yes, I believe so.
SISTER MARTHA.   It is many months
  Since his last visit.
THE SISTERS.   He is occupied
  With many things . . . Court matters . . . And the camp . . .
SISTER CLAIRE.   The busy world!

[*The nuns leave as* DE GUICHE, *now the* DUKE OF GRAMMONT, *and*
ROXANE *come silently forward and stop near the embroidery frame.*]

DE GUICHE.   And are you going to waste
  Yourself forever here in widowhood?
ROXANE.   Forever.
DE GUICHE.   Always faithful?
ROXANE.   Always.
DE GUICHE [*after a pause*].   Still,
  You have forgiven me?
ROXANE.   Since I came here.

[*There is a long silence.*]

DE GUICHE.   His was a noble soul.
ROXANE.   Noble, indeed,
  If once you knew him.
DE GUICHE.   I am sure you're right.
  We met too briefly and we spoke too little.

Is his last letter still so near your heart?

ROXANE [*indicating a ribbon around her neck*].   I wear it here, a gen-
tle talisman.

DE GUICHE.   Dead—but you love him still?

ROXANE.   Sometimes it seems
He is not dead, or only partly dead.
Our hearts were bound so close I often feel
His love, still living, hovers over me.

DE GUICHE [*after another silence*].   And does Cyrano come to see you?

ROXANE.   Yes;
Often and punctually. He is my clock,
My comfort, and my newspaper. A chair
Is put beneath this tree when the day's fair,
And there I wait with my embroidery.
The clock strikes. And in time with the last stroke,
I hear—I do not have to turn to see—
His cane upon the steps. He seats himself
And jokes about this piece of tapestry
Which never will be finished. Then
He tells me the week's gossip.

[LE BRET *appears on the steps.*]

Oh, Le Bret!
How is our friend?

LE BRET [*coming forward*].   He's very sick.

DE GUICHE.   Too bad.

ROXANE [*to* DE GUICHE].   Oh, he exaggerates.

LE BRET.   All I foretold
Has now come true: neglect and poverty
And wretched solitude. But he goes on
Fighting the hypocrites of every sort;
Exposing the sham nobles, the sham priests,
Sham heroes, shameless prudes and plagiarists,
In short, the world we know! And each attack
Wins him the malice of new enemies.

ROXANE.   But his keen sword still keeps them all at bay.
No one will ever challenge him.

DE GUICHE [*shaking his head*].   Who knows?

LE BRET.   It is not such attacks I fear. It is
Gaunt hunger, gnawing loneliness, the chill
Of stark December days, that steal into
His musty little room with wolflike steps—
These are the dread assassins that I fear.

   Each day he makes a new hole in his belt
   And grimly tightens it. His famous nose
   Is like a frail piece of old ivory.
   His wardrobe is a shabby black serge coat.
DE GUICHE. At least he's not a swaggering newly-rich.
   Don't pity him too much.
LE BRET [*with a bitter smile*]. Really, my lord!
DE GUICHE. Don't pity him too much. The man has lived
   Free in his thinking, free in every act,
   Not bought by greed nor bound by compromise.
LE BRET. My lord!
DE GUICHE. Oh yes, I know what's in your mind:
   Nothing for him, while I have everything . . .
   And yet I would be proud to press his hand. [*He bows to* ROXANE.]
   Farewell.
ROXANE. I will accompany you.

   [DE GUICHE *bows to* LE BRET *and, going toward the rear with*
   ROXANE, *stops as she ascends the steps.*]

DE GUICHE. Ah, yes,
   And strange though it may seem, I envy him.
   You see, when one has had too much success
   Too easily, one feels—though one has done
   No actual wrong—a general sense of fault,
   A thousand little lacks and grievances.
   It is not guilt and not remorse; it is
   A vague unease, a tired distrust of life.
   So, as one mounts the glittering steps of fame,
   The ermine-bordered mantle of a duke
   Drags up a cloud of dust and dry illusions,
   Just as your mourning robe sweeps these stone steps
   And drags a trail of dead, discolored leaves.
ROXANE [*with a touch of irony*]. Is this your new philosophy?
DE GUICHE. It is. [*He starts to go, then turns suddenly to* LE BRET.]
   Monsieur Le Bret, a word with you. It's true
   No one would dare to meet your friend in fight,
   But many hate the man and wish him ill.
   Yesterday at the Queen's I heard one say:
   "This Cyrano may die—by accident."
LE BRET. You heard that?
DE GUICHE. Yes. So let him stay indoors
   And go out seldom. If he's cautious—
LE BRET. He?

Cautious? The man is on his way here now!

I'll try to warn him, but—

ROXANE [*who has remained on the steps, to one of* THE SISTERS *who has approached her*].   Yes? What is it?

THE SISTER.   It's Ragueneau, Madame. He asks to see you.

ROXANE.   Let him come in. [*to* DE GUICHE *and* LE BRET]

He loves to tell his troubles.

Having set out to be a lyric writer,

He has become a singer—

LE BRET.   Bath-house-keeper—

ROXANE.   Actor—

LE BRET.   Beadle—

ROXANE.   Wig-maker—

LE BRET.   Lutanist—

ROXANE.   And heaven knows what he may be today!

RAGUENEAU [*entering rapidly*].   Ah! Madame! [*He sees* LE BRET.]

Ah! Monsieur!

ROXANE [*smiling*].   I will be back.

Meanwhile, tell your misfortunes to Le Bret.

RAGUENEAU.   But, madam—

[ROXANE *goes out with* DE GUICHE, RAGUENEAU *turns to* LE BRET.]

Perhaps it's just as well.

It would alarm her if she heard the truth.

Just now I went to see our friend. I was

A few steps from his house when he came out.

I went to meet him. As he turned the corner

I saw a window open. As he passed

Beneath the spot, a servant—someone—dropped

Either by accident or by design—

A heavy piece of wood.

LE BRET.   The nasty cowards!

RAGUENEAU.   I ran to him and saw—

LE BRET.   It's frightening!

RAGUENEAU.   Our friend, our poet, lying on the ground

Wounded, with a great hole, deep in his head.

LE BRET.   He's dead?

RAGUENEAU.   No. But, good God, I took him up

And brought him to his room. Alas, that room!

A dingy garret! You should see the place!

LE BRET.   He's suffering?

RAGUENEAU.   No. He is unconscious.

LE BRET.   You called a doctor?

RAGUENEAU.   I found one who came
  Out of pure kindness.
LE BRET.   My poor Cyrano!
  This must be broken gently to Roxane.
  What did the doctor say?
RAGUENEAU.   He shook his head and spoke about a fever,
  Something about the brain. You should have seen
  The bloody, bandaged head, the burning eyes!
  Let's go to him at once! There's no one there;
  No one to tend him. If he should get up
  He's sure to die.
LE BRET.   Hurry! Let's go this way.
  It's shorter through the chapel.

[ROXANE *appears on the steps and sees* LE BRET *pass through the colonnade leading to the chapel door.*]

ROXANE.   Monsieur Le Bret!

[LE BRET *and* RAGUENEAU *hurry away without answering.*]

I call—and Le Bret vanishes! Is this
Some new departure of poor Ragueneau? [*She descends the steps.*]
This sad September makes a lovely end.
My grief is quieted. The April gloom
Is lifted by this calm autumnal glow. [*She seats herself next to the embroidery frame.* TWO SISTERS *come out of the house, carrying a large arm-chair which they place under the tree.*]
There comes the arm-chair where he always sits,
My good and ever-faithful friend.
SISTER MARTHA.   It is
The best chair in the parlor.
ROXANE.   Thank you, sister.

[*The* TWO SISTERS *withdraw.*]

He will be here—the clock is striking now.
[*She settles herself as the clock strikes.*]
There—my embroidery . . . The clock has struck!
That's very strange. Will he be late for once?
Perhaps the sister gossiping at the gate—
Where has my thimble gone? . . . Ah, there it is!—
Is trying to convert him. [*A pause*]
Yes, she must
Be trying. He can't be much longer now.
Oh! All these falling leaves!

[*She brushes away a leaf which has fallen on the frame.*]
No, nothing could—
My scissors? . . . In my bag!—keep him from coming.
A SISTER [*appearing on the steps*].   Monsieur de Bergerac.
ROXANE [*without turning her head*].   What was I saying?

[*She goes on with her embroidery.* CYRANO *appears and the* SISTER *retires. He is extremely pale; his hat is pulled down over his eyes. He descends the steps painfully and with obvious effort; he leans heavily on his cane, for, without it, he could not stand.*]

Oh, these faint, faded colors—hard to match!
[*To* CYRANO *with an air of playful reproach*]
You're late, my friend—first time in fourteen years.

[CYRANO *has finally reached the chair and sinks into it. He replies to* ROXANE *brightly—a sprightliness in great contrast with his tortured face.*]

CYRANO.   It's too provoking! But I was detained.
ROXANE.   By whom?
CYRANO.   By an importunate visitor.
ROXANE [*absent-mindedly, continuing with her work*].   Doubtless some wicked creditor.
CYRANO.   The last
And most persistent one. He pressed me hard.
ROXANE.   But you got rid of him?
CYRANO.   Oh, yes. I said:
"Excuse me, please, but this is Saturday,
A day on which I never fail to call
Upon a certain lady. I will pay
The debt, I promise. Come back in an hour."
ROXANE [*lightly*].   Oh, let him wait much longer! I intend
To keep you with me here until it's dark.
CYRANO.   I may be forced to leave sooner than that.

[*He closes his eyes and, for a moment, is silent.* SISTER MARTHA *crosses the park, going from the chapel to the steps. Seeing her,* ROXANE *motions to her to come closer.*]

ROXANE [*to* CYRANO].   Have you been teasing Sister Martha?
CYRANO [*quickly opening his eyes*].   Yes! [*With a false gruff voice*]
Sister! Come here!

[SISTER MARTHA *approaches him.*]

Why hide those large, dark eyes?

Why keep them always bent upon the earth?
SISTER MARTHA [*smiling and raising her eyes*].   But—
      [*She sees his face and is shocked into a gesture of surprise.*]
      Oh!
CYRANO [*whispering and pointing to* ROXANE].   Hush! It is nothing.
      [*then, in a pseudo-belligerent tone*]
      Yesterday,
      Sister, I fed on meat!
SISTER MARTHA.   I'm sure you did. [*quickly and in a whisper*]
      If you will come to the refectory
      Later, I'll make you a nice bowl of soup.
      You'll come?
CYRANO.   Yes, yes.
SISTER MARTHA.   You're reasonable today.
ROXANE [*aware of the whispering but misunderstanding it*].   Is she still
      trying to convert you?
SISTER MARTHA.   No.
      Heaven forbid.
CYRANO.   It's true. You are so glib
      With pious sentiments and holy words.
      And yet you have stopped preaching to me. Yes,
      It is surprising. [*with mock anger*]
      Well, I will surprise
      You, too! [*He pauses, as if thinking of a new way to tease her and
      seeming to have found it.*]
      This very night you may—you'll never guess—
      You may—in chapel—say a prayer for me.
ROXANE [*smiling*].   Poor Sister Martha's simply stupefied.
SISTER MARTHA [*softly*].   I did not wait for you to give me leave.
      [*She goes out.*]
CYRANO [*coming to* ROXANE *and leaning over the embroidery frame*].
      How long it takes! I wonder will I see
      The end of this eternal tapestry!
ROXANE.   I have been waiting for that jest.

      [*A little breeze starts another flurry of falling leaves.*]

CYRANO.   The leaves!
ROXANE [*raising her head and looking at the distant paths*].   They are
      all gold and yellow. Watch them fall.
CYRANO.   Yes, watch them fall. It is a short-lived flight
      From branch to earth, but such a gallant one!
      Although they know that they must die and rot
      Upon the cluttered soil, they dance their way

Downward in one last ecstasy of grace.

ROXANE.   What? Melancholy? You?

CYRANO [*recovering himself*].   I? Not a bit!

ROXANE.   Well, let the dead leaves fall. Tell me the news.
Where is my Court Gazette?

CYRANO.   I'm ready.

ROXANE.   Good.

[*During the following speeches* CYRANO *grows paler and paler. He tries to make the words come lightly, but he is struggling against increasing pain.*]

CYRANO.   Saturday the nineteenth: On this day
The King lunched heartily on grape conserves
And had a touch of fever. He was bled;
The ailment was found guilty of high treason;
And the King's pulse resumed its normal beat.
The Queen's ball was on Sunday; it was lit
With more than seven hundred tall white candles.
Our troops, they say, beat John of Austria.
Four witches have been hanged. The little dog
Of Madame Athis had an enema . . .

ROXANE.   Monsieur de Bergerac! To say such things!

CYRANO.   On Monday nothing happened. Lygdamire
Took a new lover.

ROXANE.   Oh!

CYRANO [*whose face shows more and more evidences of pain*].
Tuesday, the Court
Went out to Fontainebleau. The following day
The fair Montglat said "No" to Count de Fiesque.
On Thursday the Court favorite, La Mancini,
Became the current Queen (almost!) of France.
On Friday lovely Montglat changed her mind
And said "Yes" to de Fiesque. Saturday—

[*His eyes close; his head drops. Silence. Surprised at not hearing his voice,* ROXANE *turns and observes* CYRANO *for the first time. She rises, terrified.*]

ROXANE.   He's fainted! . . . Cyrano! [*She runs toward him.*]

CYRANO [*in an indistinct voice, opening his eyes*].   What is it? What?
[*Seeing* ROXANE *bending over him, settling his hat on his head, he shrinks back frightened in his chair.*]
No! No! It's nothing! Truly! Let me be!

ROXANE.   But still—

CYRANO.   It's my old wound. The one I got
    At Arras. There are times—you know—it hurts . . .
ROXANE.   Dear friend—
CYRANO.   It's really nothing. It will pass.
    [*He makes a great effort and smiles.*]
    It *has* passed. See? The foolish pain has gone.
ROXANE [*close to him*].   Everyone bears a wound, and I bear mine.
    The old wound, never healed, is always there.
    [*She lays her hand on her breast.*]
    It still burns here; beneath his letter grown
    Yellow with time, stained with his tears and blood.

    [*Dusk creeps into the park.*]

CYRANO.   His letter! Once, long time ago, you said
    You'd let me read it.
ROXANE.   Do you really want
    To see it now?
CYRANO.   Yes. Of all days, today.
ROXANE [*giving him the little bag which hangs from her neck*].   Here.
CYRANO.   May I open it?
ROXANE.   Open, and read. [*She goes back to the embroidery frame,
    folds it, and arranges her worsteds.*]
CYRANO [*reading*].   "Roxane, farewell. It seems that I must die—"
ROXANE [*surprised*].   Aloud?
CYRANO [*continuing*].   "It might well be tonight, my own.
    My heart is heavy with unspoken love—
    And I must die too soon. Never again
    Will these infatuated eyes—"
ROXANE.   Oh, how
    You read his letter!
CYRANO.   "Feast on all your charms,
    Enjoy your smallest gesture . . . I recall
    A little way, peculiarly your own,
    You had of brushing your hand back
    Across your little forehead. So I cry—"
ROXANE.   Oh, how you read it!
CYRANO.   "So I cry 'farewell!' "

    [*It grows darker as night comes on imperceptibly.*]

ROXANE.   You read it—
CYRANO.   "Oh, my dear, my sweet, my treasure—"
ROXANE.   In such a voice—
CYRANO.   "My own true love—"

ROXANE.   A voice
    That I have heard before—sometime, somewhere.

[*She comes over to him very quietly. Then without his being aware of it, she passes behind his chair, leans noiselessly over his shoulder and looks at the letter. The darkness deepens.*]

CYRANO.   "Although I am, alas, so far away
    Never has my heart left you. For I am
    In this and even in the other world
    The one who loves you best, whose love cannot
    Be measured . . ."
ROXANE [*touching his shoulder*].   It is too dark to see.
    How can you read?

[CYRANO *is startled. He turns around, sees her very close to him and becomes alarmed. He lowers his head. There is a long silence. The dusk has deepened into night, and in the darkness* ROXANE *clasps her hands and speaks very slowly and with great gentleness.*]

And so, for fourteen years
My kind old friend who likes to chat and tease
Has played this role.
CYRANO.   Roxane!
ROXANE.   Yes, it was you!
CYRANO.   No, no, Roxane!
ROXANE.   I should have known at once!
    I should have guessed the way he spoke my name!
CYRANO.   It was not I!
ROXANE.   It was!
CYRANO.   I swear to you—
ROXANE.   I see it all—the lovely, generous lie!
    The letters—yours!
CYRANO.   No! No!
ROXANE.   The mad, sweet words—
    All yours!
CYRANO.   No! No!
ROXANE.   The voice in that dark night
    Was yours!
CYRANO.   I swear to you it never was!
ROXANE.   The very soul was yours!
CYRANO.   I never loved!
ROXANE.   You loved me always!
CYRANO.   It was someone else.
ROXANE.   You loved me!

CYRANO. No.

ROXANE. You say it softer now.

CYRANO. No, my own best beloved, I loved you not.

ROXANE. How many things long dead are born again!
Why were you silent these long fourteen years,
Since on this letter, which he never wrote,
The tears were yours!

CYRANO [*giving her back the letter*]. Ah, but the blood was his.

ROXANE. But why the noble silence? Tell me why?
And why—this day—has it been broken?

CYRANO. Why?

[LE BRET *and* RAGUENEAU *come running in out of breath.*]

LE BRET. What folly! I was sure—and here he is!

CYRANO [*smiling and sitting up*]. Of course I'm here.

LE BRET. Madame, he's killed himself
By getting up.

ROXANE. Dear God! The fainting spell!
The weakened voice! The words . . .

CYRANO. Quite true.
My gossip and Gazette were not quite finished.
Item: On Saturday, the twenty-sixth,
At dinner time, Monsieur de Bergerac
Was murdered. [*He takes off his hat, revealing his bandaged head.*]

ROXANE. Cyrano! . . . What did he say? . . .
What have they done to ruin him? . . . Oh, why?

CYRANO. "But a quick end—a worthy foeman's steel—
A pointed laughing word upon my lips
And the sword's pointed answer in my heart."
I said that once! Well, Fate has the last laugh.
Here I am trapped, struck from behind—by what?
A common block of wood! And killed by whom?
A thug, a hired cut-throat . . . I have failed
In everything in life, even in death.

RAGUENEAU. Alas, dear sir—

CYRANO [*holding out his hand*]. Ragueneau, do not weep.
Tell me, my friend, what are you doing now?

RAGUENEAU [*sobbing*]. I snuff—I snuff the candles for Molière.

CYRANO. Molière!

RAGUENEAU. But I am quitting him tomorrow.
I cannot stand it! Yesterday they played
"Scapin" with one scene he had stolen from you!

LE BRET. The whole scene—every word!

RAGUENEAU.   The famous one:
"But what the devil is he doing there?"
LE BRET.   Molière stole that!
CYRANO.   Tut! Tut! I'm glad he did.
But—speaking of the scene—how did it go?
RAGUENEAU [*through his tears*].   They laughed and laughed! I
thought they'd never stop.
CYRANO.   Yes, that has been the role I've always played:
To prompt and be forgotten. [*to* ROXANE]
You recall
That night with Christian underneath your window,
There, in the dark? That's how my life has gone.
Waiting unseen, unknown, while others mount
To endless glory and the kiss of fame.
Yet it is fair enough. And I declare
Here, on the very threshold of the tomb,
Molière has genius, and Christian had great beauty.

[*The chapel bell rings softly and the nuns pass along the path on
their way to service.*]

ROXANE [*rising and calling*].   Sister! My sister!
CYRANO [*restraining her*].   Let them go to pray.
The bell has rung. Do not go after them;
When you return I doubt I shall be here.

[*The nuns have entered the chapel, and the organ is heard.*]

My spirit needs a little harmony,
And—listen—there it is!
ROXANE.   I love you! Live!
CYRANO.   No. In the fairy tales the lady says
"I love you" and the beast becomes a prince,
As beauty banishes all ugliness.
But, though you speak the magic words, this is
No fairy tale—and I remain the same.
ROXANE.   I am the cause of your unhappiness!
I! Only I!
CYRANO.   You? Just the opposite.
I never really knew a woman's love.
My mother seldom cared to look at me.
I had no sister. I grew up to dread
A mistress or a sweetheart's mocking smile.
Still, thanks to you, I've had a cherished friend,
A woman's radiance has lit my path.

LE BRET [*pointing to the moonlight filtering through the branches*].
    Your other friend has come to visit you.
CYRANO [*smiling at the moon*].   I see her.
ROXANE.   I have loved but once—one man—
    And I must lose him twice.
CYRANO.   Tonight, Le Bret,
    I shall ascend, without machinery,
    And reach the moon at last.
ROXANE.   What do you mean?
CYRANO.   Yes, it is there that they will let me stay;
    The peerless moon will be my Paradise.
    There I will find the noble souls I love:
    Socrates . . . Galileo . . .
LE BRET [*expostulating*].   I say no!
    It is unjust and stupid! This is not
    An ending for a poet, for a mind
    So large and lofty! Such a heart and soul!
    To die like this!
CYRANO.   There goes Le Bret again,
    Still scolding, still complaining!
LE BRET [*bursting into tears*].   My dear friend . . .
CYRANO [*starting up with a wild look in his eyes*].
    "These are Cadets of Gascony!" . . . They are—
    The elementary mass . . . Ah, yes . . . the "hic" . . .
LE BRET.   A scientist—even though delirious.
CYRANO.   Copernicus said—
ROXANE.   Oh!
CYRANO.   "But what the devil—
    But what the devil is he doing there—
    There in the galley." Now, my epitaph:
              Philosopher, physician,
              Poet, fighter, and musician,
         Famous for his travels through the air;
              A fancy duellist, no less,
              A lover, too—to his distress—
        Who broke his heart pretending not to care;
    Here lies Hercule-Savinien de Cyrano de Bergerac,
    Who, thinking he was everything, was nothing.
        Ah, alas, alack!
    But pardon me, I find I cannot stay;
    The moon, you see, has come to take me home.

[*He falls back in his chair, speechless for the moment.* ROXANE's *weeping brings him back to consciousness. He looks long and longingly at her, caressing her veil.*]

I would not have you grieve one hour less
For that fine soul, the good and valiant Christian.
I only ask that when my flesh is cold,
You'll give a double meaning to this veil,
And mourn for me a little, mourning him.

ROXANE.   I promise!

[CYRANO *shivers violently but, still shaken, rises suddenly.*]

CYRANO.   No! Not here! Not in a chair!
[*They run to help him, but he waves them back.*]
No one shall hold me up!
[*He supports himself against the trunk of the tree.*]
Only the tree! [*He is silent for a moment.*]
He comes! I am already shod with stone
And gloved with lead. [*He holds himself erect.*]
Since he is on the way
I'll meet him standing—here—with sword in hand!
[*He draws his sword.*]

LE BRET.   Cyrano!

ROXANE [*almost fainting*].   Cyrano!

[*All of them shrink back, terrified.*]

CYRANO.   He sees me! Yes, he dares
To mock me for my nose, the noseless one! [*He lifts his sword.*]
What do you say? It's useless? That I know.
But who fights with assurance of success?
A man fights better when he's doomed to lose . . .
Who are you there? How many? Thousands? Ah!
I know you now, my enemies of old!
Falsehood! [*He flails the air with his sword.*]
Take that! . . . And you there, Compromise!
Prejudice! Treachery! [*He strikes out again.*]
What? Come to terms?
Never! No, never! Here is Cowardice! [*He lunges desperately.*]
And Folly, too! I know that, in the end,
You'll get me down. But, be that as it may,
I'll fight—and fight—and still go fighting on. [*He swings his sword
blindly, making wide circles, then stops, panting for breath.*]
You've robbed me of the laurel and the rose,
Glory and love . . . Take them! Take everything!

But there is one thing that you shall not have;
One thing I take with me. And when, tonight,
I enter God's great house, I shall bend low,
And, bowing, sweep the threshold's heavenly blue
With something which—in spite of you—I wear . . .
[*He raises his sword, about to spring forward.*]
And that thing is— [*The sword clatters from his hand. He totters
and falls into the arms of* LE BRET *and* RAGUENEAU.]
ROXANE [*bending over him and gently kissing him on the forehead*].
   That is—?
CYRANO [*opening his eyes, recognizing her, and smiling contentedly*].
   My stainless plume:
   My pride, my pose, my lifelong masquerade.

[*The curtain falls.*]

DOVER·THRIFT·EDITIONS

POETRY

THE CONGO AND OTHER POEMS, Vachel Lindsay. 96pp. 0-486-27272-9

EVANGELINE AND OTHER POEMS, Henry Wadsworth Longfellow. 64pp. 0-486-28255-4

FAVORITE POEMS, Henry Wadsworth Longfellow. 96pp. 0-486-27273-7

"TO HIS COY MISTRESS" AND OTHER POEMS, Andrew Marvell. 64pp. 0-486-29544-3

SPOON RIVER ANTHOLOGY, Edgar Lee Masters. 144pp. 0-486-27275-3

SELECTED POEMS, Claude McKay. 80pp. 0-486-40876-0

RENASCENCE AND OTHER POEMS, Edna St. Vincent Millay. 64pp. (Not available in Europe or the United Kingdom) 0-486-26873-X

SELECTED POEMS, John Milton. 128pp. 0-486-27554-X

CIVIL WAR POETRY: An Anthology, Paul Negri (ed.). 128pp. 0-486-29883-3

ENGLISH VICTORIAN POETRY: AN ANTHOLOGY, Paul Negri (ed.). 256pp. 0-486-40425-0

GREAT SONNETS, Paul Negri (ed.). 96pp. 0-486-28052-7

THE RAVEN AND OTHER FAVORITE POEMS, Edgar Allan Poe. 64pp. 0-486-26685-0

ESSAY ON MAN AND OTHER POEMS, Alexander Pope. 128pp. 0-486-28053-5

EARLY POEMS, Ezra Pound. 80pp. (Available in U.S. only.) 0-486-28745-9

GREAT POEMS BY AMERICAN WOMEN: An Anthology, Susan L. Rattiner (ed.). 224pp. (Available in U.S. only.) 0-486-40164-2

GOBLIN MARKET AND OTHER POEMS, Christina Rossetti. 64pp. 0-486-28055-1

CHICAGO POEMS, Carl Sandburg. 80pp. 0-486-28057-8

CORNHUSKERS, Carl Sandburg. 157pp. 0-486-41409-4

COMPLETE SONNETS, William Shakespeare. 80pp. 0-486-26686-9

SELECTED POEMS, Percy Bysshe Shelley. 128pp. 0-486-27558-2

AFRICAN-AMERICAN POETRY: An Anthology, 1773–1930, Joan R. Sherman (ed.). 96pp. 0-486-29604-0

100 BEST-LOVED POEMS, Philip Smith (ed.). 96pp. 0-486-28553-7

NATIVE AMERICAN SONGS AND POEMS: An Anthology, Brian Swann (ed.). 64pp. 0-486-29450-1

SELECTED POEMS, Alfred Lord Tennyson. 112pp. 0-486-27282-6

AENEID, Vergil (Publius Vergilius Maro). 256pp. 0-486-28749-1

CHRISTMAS CAROLS: COMPLETE VERSES, Shane Weller (ed.). 64pp. 0-486-27397-0

GREAT LOVE POEMS, Shane Weller (ed.). 128pp. 0-486-27284-2

CIVIL WAR POETRY AND PROSE, Walt Whitman. 96pp. 0-486-28507-3

SELECTED POEMS, Walt Whitman. 128pp. 0-486-26878-0

THE BALLAD OF READING GAOL AND OTHER POEMS, Oscar Wilde. 64pp. 0-486-27072-6

EARLY POEMS, William Carlos Williams. 64pp. (Available in U.S. only.) 0-486-29294-0

FAVORITE POEMS, William Wordsworth. 80pp. 0-486-27073-4

WORLD WAR ONE BRITISH POETS: Brooke, Owen, Sassoon, Rosenberg, and Others, Candace Ward (ed.). (Available in U.S. only.) 0-486-29568-0

EARLY POEMS, William Butler Yeats. 128pp. 0-486-27808-5

"EASTER, 1916" AND OTHER POEMS, William Butler Yeats. 80pp. (Not available in Europe or United Kingdom.) 0-486-29771-3

FICTION

FLATLAND: A ROMANCE OF MANY DIMENSIONS, Edwin A. Abbott. 96pp. 0-486-27263-X

SHORT STORIES, Louisa May Alcott. 64pp. 0-486-29063-8

WINESBURG, OHIO, Sherwood Anderson. 160pp. 0-486-28269-4

PERSUASION, Jane Austen. 224pp. 0-486-29555-9

PRIDE AND PREJUDICE, Jane Austen. 272pp. 0-486-28473-5

SENSE AND SENSIBILITY, Jane Austen. 272pp. 0-486-29049-2

LOOKING BACKWARD, Edward Bellamy. 160pp. 0-486-29038-7

BEOWULF, Beowulf (trans. by R. K. Gordon). 64pp. 0-486-27264-8

CIVIL WAR STORIES, Ambrose Bierce. 128pp. 0-486-28038-1

WUTHERING HEIGHTS, Emily Brontë. 256pp. 0-486-29256-8

THE THIRTY-NINE STEPS, John Buchan. 96pp. 0-486-28201-5

TARZAN OF THE APES, Edgar Rice Burroughs. 224pp. (Not available in Europe or United Kingdom.) 0-486-29570-2

ALICE'S ADVENTURES IN WONDERLAND, Lewis Carroll. 96pp. 0-486-27543-4

THROUGH THE LOOKING-GLASS, Lewis Carroll. 128pp. 0-486-40878-7

MY ÁNTONIA, Willa Cather. 176pp. 0-486-28240-6

O PIONEERS!, Willa Cather. 128pp. 0-486-27785-2

FIVE GREAT SHORT STORIES, Anton Chekhov. 96pp. 0-486-26463-7

TALES OF CONJURE AND THE COLOR LINE, Charles Waddell Chesnutt. 128pp. 0-486-40426-9

FAVORITE FATHER BROWN STORIES, G. K. Chesterton. 96pp. 0-486-27545-0

THE AWAKENING, Kate Chopin. 128pp. 0-486-27786-0

A PAIR OF SILK STOCKINGS AND OTHER STORIES, Kate Chopin. 64pp. 0-486-29264-9

HEART OF DARKNESS, Joseph Conrad. 80pp. 0-486-26464-5

LORD JIM, Joseph Conrad. 256pp. 0-486-40650-4

THE SECRET SHARER AND OTHER STORIES, Joseph Conrad. 128pp. 0-486-27546-9

THE "LITTLE REGIMENT" AND OTHER CIVIL WAR STORIES, Stephen Crane. 80pp. 0-486-29557-5

THE OPEN BOAT AND OTHER STORIES, Stephen Crane. 128pp. 0-486-27547-7

THE RED BADGE OF COURAGE, Stephen Crane. 112pp. 0-486-26465-3

MOLL FLANDERS, Daniel Defoe. 256pp. 0-486-29093-X

ROBINSON CRUSOE, Daniel Defoe. 288pp. 0-486-40427-7

A CHRISTMAS CAROL, Charles Dickens. 80pp. 0-486-26865-9

THE CRICKET ON THE HEARTH AND OTHER CHRISTMAS STORIES, Charles Dickens. 128pp. 0-486-28039-X

A TALE OF TWO CITIES, Charles Dickens. 304pp. 0-486-40651-2

THE DOUBLE, Fyodor Dostoyevsky. 128pp. 0-486-29572-9

THE GAMBLER, Fyodor Dostoyevsky. 112pp. 0-486-29081-6

NOTES FROM THE UNDERGROUND, Fyodor Dostoyevsky. 96pp. 0-486-27053-X

THE ADVENTURE OF THE DANCING MEN AND OTHER STORIES, Sir Arthur Conan Doyle. 80pp. 0-486-29558-3

THE HOUND OF THE BASKERVILLES, Arthur Conan Doyle. 128pp. 0-486-28214-7

THE LOST WORLD, Arthur Conan Doyle. 176pp. 0-486-40060-3

DOVER·THRIFT·EDITIONS

FICTION

A JOURNAL OF THE PLAGUE YEAR, Daniel Defoe. 192pp. 0-486-41919-3
SIX GREAT SHERLOCK HOLMES STORIES, Sir Arthur Conan Doyle. 112pp. 0-486-27055-6
SHORT STORIES, Theodore Dreiser. 112pp. 0-486-28215-5
SILAS MARNER, George Eliot. 160pp. 0-486-29246-0
JOSEPH ANDREWS, Henry Fielding. 288pp. 0-486-41588-0
THIS SIDE OF PARADISE, F. Scott Fitzgerald. 208pp. 0-486-28999-0
"THE DIAMOND AS BIG AS THE RITZ" AND OTHER STORIES, F. Scott Fitzgerald. 0-486-29991-0
MADAME BOVARY, Gustave Flaubert. 256pp. 0-486-29257-6
THE REVOLT OF "MOTHER" AND OTHER STORIES, Mary E. Wilkins Freeman. 128pp. 0-486-40428-5
A ROOM WITH A VIEW, E. M. Forster. 176pp. (Available in U.S. only.) 0-486-28467-0
WHERE ANGELS FEAR TO TREAD, E. M. Forster. 128pp. (Available in U.S. only.) 0-486-27791-7
THE IMMORALIST, André Gide. 112pp. (Available in U.S. only.) 0-486-29237-1
HERLAND, Charlotte Perkins Gilman. 128pp. 0-486-40429-3
"THE YELLOW WALLPAPER" AND OTHER STORIES, Charlotte Perkins Gilman. 80pp. 0-486-29857-4
THE OVERCOAT AND OTHER STORIES, Nikolai Gogol. 112pp. 0-486-27057-2
CHELKASH AND OTHER STORIES, Maxim Gorky. 64pp. 0-486-40652-0
GREAT GHOST STORIES, John Grafton (ed.). 112pp. 0-486-27270-2
DETECTION BY GASLIGHT, Douglas G. Greene (ed.). 272pp. 0-486-29928-7
THE MABINOGION, Lady Charlotte E. Guest. 192pp. 0-486-29541-9
"THE FIDDLER OF THE REELS" AND OTHER SHORT STORIES, Thomas Hardy. 80pp. 0-486-29960-0
THE LUCK OF ROARING CAMP AND OTHER STORIES, Bret Harte. 96pp. 0-486-27271-0
THE HOUSE OF THE SEVEN GABLES, Nathaniel Hawthorne. 272pp. 0-486-40882-5
THE SCARLET LETTER, Nathaniel Hawthorne. 192pp. 0-486-28048-9
YOUNG GOODMAN BROWN AND OTHER STORIES, Nathaniel Hawthorne. 128pp. 0-486-27060-2
THE GIFT OF THE MAGI AND OTHER SHORT STORIES, O. Henry. 96pp. 0-486-27061-0
THE ASPERN PAPERS, Henry James. 112pp. 0-486-41922-3
THE BEAST IN THE JUNGLE AND OTHER STORIES, Henry James. 128pp. 0-486-27552-3
DAISY MILLER, Henry James. 64pp. 0-486-28773-4
THE TURN OF THE SCREW, Henry James. 96pp. 0-486-26684-2
WASHINGTON SQUARE, Henry James. 176pp. 0-486-40431-5
THE COUNTRY OF THE POINTED FIRS, Sarah Orne Jewett. 96pp. 0-486-28196-5
THE AUTOBIOGRAPHY OF AN EX-COLORED MAN, James Weldon Johnson. 112pp. 0-486-28512-X
DUBLINERS, James Joyce. 160pp. 0-486-26870-5
A PORTRAIT OF THE ARTIST AS A YOUNG MAN, James Joyce. 192pp. 0-486-28050-0
THE METAMORPHOSIS AND OTHER STORIES, Franz Kafka. 96pp. 0-486-29030-1
THE MAN WHO WOULD BE KING AND OTHER STORIES, Rudyard Kipling. 128pp. 0-486-28051-9
YOU KNOW ME AL, Ring Lardner. 128pp. 0-486-28513-8
SELECTED SHORT STORIES, D. H. Lawrence. 128pp. 0-486-27794-1
THE CALL OF THE WILD, Jack London. 64pp. 0-486-26472-6
FIVE GREAT SHORT STORIES, Jack London. 96pp. 0-486-27063-7
THE SEA-WOLF, Jack London. 248pp. 0-486-41108-7
WHITE FANG, Jack London. 160pp. 0-486-26968-X
DEATH IN VENICE, Thomas Mann. 96pp. (Available in U.S. only.) 0-486-28714-9
THE NECKLACE AND OTHER SHORT STORIES, Guy de Maupassant. 128pp. 0-486-27064-5
BARTLEBY AND BENITO CERENO, Herman Melville. 112pp. 0-486-26473-4
THE OIL JAR AND OTHER STORIES, Luigi Pirandello. 96pp. 0-486-28459-X
THE GOLD-BUG AND OTHER TALES, Edgar Allan Poe. 128pp. 0-486-26875-6
TALES OF TERROR AND DETECTION, Edgar Allan Poe. 96pp. 0-486-28744-0

DOVER·THRIFT·EDITIONS

FICTION

THE QUEEN OF SPADES AND OTHER STORIES, Alexander Pushkin. 128pp. 0-486-28054-3

THE STORY OF AN AFRICAN FARM, Olive Schreiner. 256pp. 0-486-40165-0

FRANKENSTEIN, Mary Shelley. 176pp. 0-486-28211-2

THE JUNGLE, Upton Sinclair. 320pp. (Available in U.S. only.) 0-486-41923-1

THREE LIVES, Gertrude Stein. 176pp. (Available in U.S. only.) 0-486-28059-4

THE BODY SNATCHER AND OTHER TALES, Robert Louis Stevenson. 80pp. 0-486-41924-X

THE STRANGE CASE OF DR. JEKYLL AND MR. HYDE, Robert Louis Stevenson. 64pp. 0-486-26688-5

TREASURE ISLAND, Robert Louis Stevenson. 160pp. 0-486-27559-0

GULLIVER'S TRAVELS, Jonathan Swift. 240pp. 0-486-29273-8

THE KREUTZER SONATA AND OTHER SHORT STORIES, Leo Tolstoy. 144pp. 0-486-27805-0

THE WARDEN, Anthony Trollope. 176pp. 0-486-40076-X

FATHERS AND SONS, Ivan Turgenev. 176pp. 0-486-0073-5

ADVENTURES OF HUCKLEBERRY FINN, Mark Twain. 224pp. 0-486-28061-6

THE ADVENTURES OF TOM SAWYER, Mark Twain. 192pp. 0-486-40077-8

THE MYSTERIOUS STRANGER AND OTHER STORIES, Mark Twain. 128pp. 0-486-27069-6

HUMOROUS STORIES AND SKETCHES, Mark Twain. 80pp. 0-486-29279-7

AROUND THE WORLD IN EIGHTY DAYS, Jules Verne. 160pp. 0-486-41111-7

CANDIDE, Voltaire (François-Marie Arouet). 112pp. 0-486-26689-3

GREAT SHORT STORIES BY AMERICAN WOMEN, Candace Ward (ed.). 192pp. 0-486-28776-9

"THE COUNTRY OF THE BLIND" AND OTHER SCIENCE-FICTION STORIES, H. G. Wells. 160pp. (Not available in Europe or United Kingdom.) 0-486-29569-9

THE ISLAND OF DR. MOREAU, H. G. Wells. 112pp. (Not available in Europe or United Kingdom.) 0-486-29027-1

THE INVISIBLE MAN, H. G. Wells. 112pp. (Not available in Europe or United Kingdom.) 0-486-27071-8

THE TIME MACHINE, H. G. Wells. 80pp. (Not available in Europe or United Kingdom.) 0-486-28472-7

THE WAR OF THE WORLDS, H. G. Wells. 160pp. (Not available in Europe or United Kingdom.) 0-486-29506-0

ETHAN FROME, Edith Wharton. 96pp. 0-486-26690-7

SHORT STORIES, Edith Wharton. 128pp. 0-486-28235-X

THE AGE OF INNOCENCE, Edith Wharton. 288pp. 0-486-29803-5

THE PICTURE OF DORIAN GRAY, Oscar Wilde. 192pp. 0-486-27807-7

JACOB'S ROOM, Virginia Woolf. 144pp. (Not available in Europe or United Kingdom.) 0-486-40109-X

MONDAY OR TUESDAY: Eight Stories, Virginia Woolf. 64pp. (Not available in Europe or United Kingdom.) 0-486-29453-6

NONFICTION

POETICS, Aristotle. 64pp. 0-486-29577-X

POLITICS, Aristotle. 368pp. 0-486-41424-8

NICOMACHEAN ETHICS, Aristotle. 256pp. 0-486-40096-4

MEDITATIONS, Marcus Aurelius. 128pp. 0-486-29823-X

THE LAND OF LITTLE RAIN, Mary Austin. 96pp. 0-486-29037-9

THE DEVIL'S DICTIONARY, Ambrose Bierce. 144pp. 0-486-27542-6

THE ANALECTS, Confucius. 128pp. 0-486-28484-0

CONFESSIONS OF AN ENGLISH OPIUM EATER, Thomas De Quincey. 80pp. 0-486-28742-4

THE SOULS OF BLACK FOLK, W. E. B. Du Bois. 176pp. 0-486-28041-1

DOVER·THRIFT·EDITIONS

NONFICTION

NARRATIVE OF THE LIFE OF FREDERICK DOUGLASS, Frederick Douglass. 96pp. 0-486-28499-9

SELF-RELIANCE AND OTHER ESSAYS, Ralph Waldo Emerson. 128pp. 0-486-27790-9

THE LIFE OF OLAUDAH EQUIANO, OR GUSTAVUS VASSA, THE AFRICAN, Olaudah Equiano. 192pp. 0-486-40661-X

THE AUTOBIOGRAPHY OF BENJAMIN FRANKLIN, Benjamin Franklin. 144pp. 0-486-29073-5

TOTEM AND TABOO, Sigmund Freud. 176pp. (Not available in Europe or United Kingdom.) 0-486-40434-X

LOVE: A Book of Quotations, Herb Galewitz (ed.). 64pp. 0-486-40004-2

PRAGMATISM, William James. 128pp. 0-486-28270-8

THE STORY OF MY LIFE, Helen Keller. 80pp. 0-486-29249-5

TAO TE CHING, Lao Tze. 112pp. 0-486-29792-6

GREAT SPEECHES, Abraham Lincoln. 112pp. 0-486-26872-1

THE PRINCE, Niccolò Machiavelli. 80pp. 0-486-27274-5

THE SUBJECTION OF WOMEN, John Stuart Mill. 112pp. 0-486-29601-6

SELECTED ESSAYS, Michel de Montaigne. 96pp. 0-486-29109-X

UTOPIA, Sir Thomas More. 96pp. 0-486-29583-4

BEYOND GOOD AND EVIL: Prelude to a Philosophy of the Future, Friedrich Nietzsche. 176pp. 0-486-29868-X

THE BIRTH OF TRAGEDY, Friedrich Nietzsche. 96pp. 0-486-28515-4

COMMON SENSE, Thomas Paine. 64pp. 0-486-29602-4

SYMPOSIUM AND PHAEDRUS, Plato. 96pp. 0-486-27798-4

THE TRIAL AND DEATH OF SOCRATES: Four Dialogues, Plato. 128pp. 0-486-27066-1

A MODEST PROPOSAL AND OTHER SATIRICAL WORKS, Jonathan Swift. 64pp. 0-486-28759-9

CIVIL DISOBEDIENCE AND OTHER ESSAYS, Henry David Thoreau. 96pp. 0-486-27563-9

WALDEN; OR, LIFE IN THE WOODS, Henry David Thoreau. 224pp. 0-486-28495-6

NARRATIVE OF SOJOURNER TRUTH, Sojourner Truth. 80pp. 0-486-29899-X

THE THEORY OF THE LEISURE CLASS, Thorstein Veblen. 256pp. 0-486-28062-4

DE PROFUNDIS, Oscar Wilde. 64pp. 0-486-29308-4

OSCAR WILDE'S WIT AND WISDOM: A Book of Quotations, Oscar Wilde. 64pp. 0-486-40146-4

UP FROM SLAVERY, Booker T. Washington. 160pp. 0-486-28738-6

A VINDICATION OF THE RIGHTS OF WOMAN, Mary Wollstonecraft. 224pp. 0-486-29036-0

PLAYS

PROMETHEUS BOUND, Aeschylus. 64pp. 0-486-28762-9

THE ORESTEIA TRILOGY: Agamemnon, The Libation-Bearers and The Furies, Aeschylus. 160pp. 0-486-29242-8

LYSISTRATA, Aristophanes. 64pp. 0-486-28225-2

WHAT EVERY WOMAN KNOWS, James Barrie. 80pp. (Not available in Europe or United Kingdom.) 0-486-29578-8

THE CHERRY ORCHARD, Anton Chekhov. 64pp. 0-486-26682-6

THE SEA GULL, Anton Chekhov. 64pp. 0-486-40656-3

THE THREE SISTERS, Anton Chekhov. 64pp. 0-486-27544-2

UNCLE VANYA, Anton Chekhov. 64pp. 0-486-40159-6

THE WAY OF THE WORLD, William Congreve. 80pp. 0-486-27787-9

BACCHAE, Euripides. 64pp. 0-486-29580-X

MEDEA, Euripides. 64pp. 0-486-27548-5

DOVER·THRIFT·EDITIONS

PLAYS

Life Is a Dream, Pedro Calderón de la Barca. 96pp. 0-486-42124-4
H. M. S. Pinafore, William Schwenck Gilbert. 64pp. 0-486-41114-1
The Mikado, William Schwenck Gilbert. 64pp. 0-486-27268-0
She Stoops to Conquer, Oliver Goldsmith. 80pp. 0-486-26867-5
The Lower Depths, Maxim Gorky. 80pp. 0-486-41115-X
A Doll's House, Henrik Ibsen. 80pp. 0-486-27062-9
Ghosts, Henrik Ibsen. 64pp. 0-486-29852-3
Hedda Gabler, Henrik Ibsen. 80pp. 0-486-26469-6
Peer Gynt, Henrik Ibsen. 144pp. 0-486-42686-6
The Wild Duck, Henrik Ibsen. 96pp. 0-486-41116-8
Volpone, Ben Jonson. 112pp. 0-486-28049-7
Dr. Faustus, Christopher Marlowe. 64pp. 0-486-28208-2
Tamburlaine, Christopher Marlowe. 128pp. 0-486-42125-2
The Imaginary Invalid, Molière. 96pp. 0-486-43789-2
The Misanthrope, Molière. 64pp. 0-486-27065-3
Right You Are, If You Think You Are, Luigi Pirandello. 64pp. (Not available in Europe or United Kingdom.) 0-486-29576-1
Six Characters in Search of an Author, Luigi Pirandello. 64pp. (Not available in Europe or United Kingdom.) 0-486-29992-9
Phèdre, Jean Racine. 64pp. 0-486-41927-4
Hands Around, Arthur Schnitzler. 64pp. 0-486-28724-6
Antony and Cleopatra, William Shakespeare. 128pp. 0-486-40062-X
As You Like It, William Shakespeare. 80pp. 0-486-40432-3
Hamlet, William Shakespeare. 128pp. 0-486-27278-8
Henry IV, William Shakespeare. 96pp. 0-486-29584-2
Julius Caesar, William Shakespeare. 80pp. 0-486-26876-4
King Lear, William Shakespeare. 112pp. 0-486-28058-6
Love's Labour's Lost, William Shakespeare. 64pp. 0-486-41929-0
Macbeth, William Shakespeare. 96pp. 0-486-27802-6
Measure for Measure, William Shakespeare. 96pp. 0-486-40889-2
The Merchant of Venice, William Shakespeare. 96pp. 0-486-28492-1
A Midsummer Night's Dream, William Shakespeare. 80pp. 0-486-27067-X
Much Ado About Nothing, William Shakespeare. 80pp. 0-486-28272-4
Othello, William Shakespeare. 112pp. 0-486-29097-2
Richard III, William Shakespeare. 112pp. 0-486-28747-5
Romeo and Juliet, William Shakespeare. 96pp. 0-486-27557-4
The Taming of the Shrew, William Shakespeare. 96pp. 0-486-29765-9
The Tempest, William Shakespeare. 96pp. 0-486-40658-X
Twelfth Night; or, What You Will, William Shakespeare. 80pp. 0-486-29290-8
Arms and the Man, George Bernard Shaw. 80pp. (Not available in Europe or United Kingdom.) 0-486-26476-9
Heartbreak House, George Bernard Shaw. 128pp. (Not available in Europe or United Kingdom.) 0-486-29291-6
Pygmalion, George Bernard Shaw. 96pp. (Available in U.S. only.) 0-486-28222-8
The Rivals, Richard Brinsley Sheridan. 96pp. 0-486-40433-1
The School for Scandal, Richard Brinsley Sheridan. 96pp. 0-486-26687-7
Antigone, Sophocles. 64pp. 0-486-27804-2
Oedipus at Colonus, Sophocles. 64pp. 0-486-40659-8
Oedipus Rex, Sophocles. 64pp. 0-486-26877-2

DOVER · THRIFT · EDITIONS

PLAYS

ELECTRA, Sophocles. 64pp. 0-486-28482-4

MISS JULIE, August Strindberg. 64pp. 0-486-27281-8

THE PLAYBOY OF THE WESTERN WORLD AND RIDERS TO THE SEA, J. M. Synge. 80pp. 0-486-27562-0

THE DUCHESS OF MALFI, John Webster. 96pp. 0-486-40660-1

THE IMPORTANCE OF BEING EARNEST, Oscar Wilde. 64pp. 0-486-26478-5

LADY WINDERMERE'S FAN, Oscar Wilde. 64pp. 0-486-40078-6

BOXED SETS

FAVORITE JANE AUSTEN NOVELS: *Pride and Prejudice*, *Sense and Sensibility* and *Persuasion* (Complete and Unabridged), Jane Austen. 800pp. 0-486-29748-9

BEST WORKS OF MARK TWAIN: Four Books, Dover. 624pp. 0-486-40226-6

EIGHT GREAT GREEK TRAGEDIES: Six Books, Dover. 480pp. 0-486-40203-7

FIVE GREAT ENGLISH ROMANTIC POETS, Dover. 496pp. 0-486-27893-X

GREAT AFRICAN-AMERICAN WRITERS: Seven Books, Dover. 704pp. 0-486-29995-3

GREAT WOMEN POETS: 4 Complete Books, Dover. 256pp. (Available in U.S. only.) 0-486-28388-7

MASTERPIECES OF RUSSIAN LITERATURE: Seven Books, Dover. 880pp. 0-486-40665-2

SIX GREAT AMERICAN POETS: Poems by Poe, Dickinson, Whitman, Longfellow, Frost, and Millay, Dover. 512pp. (Available in U.S. only.) 0-486-27425-X

FAVORITE NOVELS AND STORIES: Four Complete Books, Jack London. 568pp. 0-486-42216-X

FIVE GREAT SCIENCE FICTION NOVELS, H. G. Wells. 640pp. 0-486-43978-X

FIVE GREAT PLAYS OF SHAKESPEARE, Dover. 496pp. 0-486-27892-1

TWELVE PLAYS BY SHAKESPEARE, William Shakespeare. 1,173pp. 0-486-44336-1

All books complete and unabridged. All 5³⁄₁₆" x 8¼", paperbound. Available at your book dealer, online at **www.doverpublications.com**, or by writing to Dept. GI, Dover Publications, Inc., 31 East 2nd Street, Mineola, NY 11501. For current price information or for free catalogs (please indicate field of interest), write to Dover Publications or log on to **www.doverpublications.com** and see every Dover book in print. Dover publishes more than 500 books each year on science, elementary and advanced mathematics, biology, music, art, literary history, social sciences, and other areas.